REVIATHAN

BOOK 1 : THE SPARKS

by Nadia Joynson

First published in France in 2018

TO THE WORLD'S FUTURE INNOVATORS
MAY YOUR CREATIONS BRING YOU JOY
AND HELP HUMANITY TO FIND PEACE

With sincerest gratitude to my companion
Vincent and my brother Leigh for their love and support

CONTENTS

Preface - The Birth of Reviathan
Chapter 1 - Bethanor The Innovator
Chapter 2 - The Hideout
Chapter 3 - Sector Four
Chapter 4 - The Jade Lady
Chapter 5 - Discovering New Earth
Chapter 6 - The Experiment
Chapter 7 - The Return of The Recluse
Chapter 8 - Morphing The Aurora Belt

Preface

The Birth of Reviathan

In my mind's eye, the world no longer exists as it once did. No multitudes of cars streaming along the highways to work in the morning, no mail man bringing letters by hand, no queues in the supermarkets. In fact supermarkets no longer exist, no drugstores, no malls. No, we had to start again, but not quite from the beginning....

This is the world in 2093. A world in which the meaning of why we do things comes first; a world where being together is more important than being right; a world where we can all decide how things should happen by co-creating them. This is a world after the environmental devastation of 2027, where the human race needed to choose six land masses to save. The continents were being ravaged by colossal tsunamis and earthquakes. Earth as we knew it quickly became uninhabitable, barren or inundated by a toxic and silt-filled sludge for as far as the eye can see. Fire swept over acres of forest in the wake of the earthquakes. Humans and animals alike fled for their lives leaving just a pungent smell of devastation behind them.

It will take hundreds, maybe thousands of years of nurturing and state of the art technology to repair. But a New Earth will return. We pledged that it will be so. We will once again see fields and forests, lakes and magnificent mountains rise above the skyline, majestic as they dry and regenerate, allowing life to once again flourish.

All that is left now of the human race, six tribes of several hundred thousand people, live interspersed among the chosen lands (the Spark, Star, Sunset, Stream, Season and Snow tribes). Their lives peaceful and generous as they evolve into a new way of living together, once again in harmony with their universe, never again abusing the energy fields and nature itself that supports them. They ultimately don't need to, since they discovered new ways of doing things with their highly evolved gifts. Finally we accepted to be conscious of our impact on the world around us. Ultimately, life made us choose.

Chapter One

Bethanor The Innovator

The light coming from the enormous bay window gently flooded across the floor of the room where Bethanor was encircled with objects as precious and obscure, as they were rare. Leant back in his chair in deep reflection, he suddenly sprang forwards and lifted a strange contraption into his field of vision, turning it fervently in different directions. His piercing green eyes focused intently on scrutinising every tiny aspect of the small, mechanical object in front of him. He clicked levers, twisted knobs and opened the back gently to reveal an unravelling of multi-coloured wires. As he removed each element rigorously, gazing deeply to understand its position and function, he continued to think about the object's potential purpose.

The Seasons Tribe regularly brought relics to the Sparks tribe. They would find them in the permaculture sectors that they were excavating to produce new food sources, and they loved to offer them as gifts to the children for them to disassemble. Unless of course they were objects that had never been seen before. These were taken to high security laboratories and analysed with deep respect and care in order for the general register of knowledge to be enriched with any new information they provided. Even better if the object contained molecules that had never been seen before. Although a rare occurrence now, sometimes Reviathan did receive 'new' elements which helped them to further understand their environment and also to innovate some amazing and highly advanced technologies. After all it was part of the Spark tribe's nature, they were creators, innovators, before all things. In doing so they were in an excellent position to intuitively feel what variety of elements could be combined and for what purpose.

Bethanor was a Spark, raised according to tradition by decomposing and reassembling object after object with the ultimate goal of understanding the composition and purpose of all things. What was particular about them was that they could do this right down to their minutest form, as pure molecules. You could see pulses of energy and colours in front of them as each aspect would separate out to be analysed and recorded as a reference within their energy fields. Having registered the new reference, they would have the ability to call on that element, recomposing any item they choose. This was a gift that the Sparks Tribe had developed in order to survive the environmental cataclysm. They had needed to recompose materials and provisions from the few remaining elements available to them in order to feed and house the thousands of people stranded. Much of the Earth's natural resources had been destroyed.

As intellectuals and engineers in the days prior to the great environmental overhaul, they spent hours of frustration trying to forcefully build tools and innovations, many of which had no real use. Once they had developed these fusioning capabilities, they realised that there were simpler ways to innovate and that their struggle would be over. The universe had left them clues as to the nature of all things and once they started to understand the linkages between them, the position of each of them began to reveal itself as part of one big perfect whole. Everything had a purpose, everything had a place within the natural realm, including humans. Their abilities grew and so creating then became a sacred purpose.

The fun really began as they used their abilities to put things back together again. The air would fill with swirls of energy and combusting sparks of silver or white light. This was how they earned their name, the Sparks. Children from the Sparks Tribe would watch, fascinated, as their parents would perform tricks of all types to amuse them and also share knowledge with their Youngers. For the Sparks were known to love to play and they used experimentation as the basis for learning. This kept the Youngers lively and engaged whilst also enjoying moments of connection together. Daily life was like one permanent magic show!

But Bethanor was bored. It was rare at the age of 17 that anyone found an object that he did not know how to disassemble and reassemble. His dissembling skills were widely known to be exemplary, but he was not yet allowed to create spontaneously for he had not completed his rite of passage. At least he was not allowed to create according to the knowledge of his parents... His carer, an elder who was reading quietly in the corner of the room was almost falling asleep. He had accompanied Bethanor for many moons and knew that he liked to be independent in his research so he gave him plenty of space. Bethanor was becoming restless, although his carer did not notice. He spun around the object he had been analysing. He carefully decomposed the central core and with two or three tweaks he began to pick up noise from the surrounding area. The radio identified a form within a 500 metre range of his current position and through the sound pulsator, he could hear approaching footsteps.

Sparks flew and energy swirled in the air as Bethanor decomposed and recomposed matter, quickly walling himself into a cavity of the main wall of the room. The metal panel was exactly the same as the two adjacent sections. In an instant, he was nowhere to be seen.

The footsteps became louder and the door slid open. A tall, elegant woman entered the room and immediately paused to look around. Her eyes sparkling, she scanned the room for Bethanor's presence. A wide smile swept across Zenalis's face, she touched each panel of the room gently, concentrating on feeling its composition. As she approached the fourth panel she laughed loudly.

"There you are!" she sighed as the panel in front of Bethanor dissolved into a swirl of energy.

Bethanor's eyes were twinkling with mischief as he also laughed at having been discovered so easily by his loving and very astute mother.

Zenalis was a highly intelligent and diligent member of the High Council of Innovation, one of the central institutions in Reviathan. Her abilities to encourage participation and creativity in some of the most memorable creations of the post environmental cataclysm era had been highly commended. She was a leader of co-creation. This was a very important role for the community, but like all Sparks, she never lost her love of play.

The mood was much lighter now and the two connected briefly for a moment of reuniting. Zenalis had been away for several days working on a strategic project. The Sparks Tribe were at a very delicate phase of their evolution. They where agreeing on the criteria which would be used to decide whether each of their creations would raise rather than lower humanity's well-being. Once this was in place, Sparks would be free to express themselves through any innovation that they felt deeply was trying to emerge for the greater good.

"I have come to remind you of your rite of passage before the Committee. Do you already have in mind the innovation that you will present to them? I would like you to know that whatever you chose, I am very proud of you," she said lovingly.

Bethanor was taken slightly aback. Was it so soon? At this moment, he would at last be recognised for all of his innovative capacities.

"When?" he asked.

"In three week's time," replied Zenalis, "when the stars align to enable ingenuity to flourish for the benefit of all."

"Three weeks," thought Bethanor "so I still have time to do some research."

"All is well mother," Bethanor replied.

"It seems like yesterday that, as a little boy you were deeply focused on your very first decompositions," she continued. "Just a very simple crystal formation but you did it with so much care and attention to detail, and you were not even two years old at the time! You have come so far."

Bethanor blushed. He was 17 years old and didn't need reminding of his early fumbling years. His mother kissed his forehead lovingly and turned to leave the room. "We will discuss with your father on this eve," she called behind her as she proceeded to leave the room. "He will be delighted by your enthusiasm. You are truly coming of age and your wisdom will accompany you. Let it be so."

The rite of passage process itself sounded boring to Bethanor and he imagined the tedious hours of listening to everyone else before he would finally have his moment to speak.

"Why can't we make these gatherings fun?" he sighed.

Still it was an opportunity to shine and he rarely missed these. What would he need to do to complete his project?

Bethanor himself was an aspiring artist. He created his works from different medias, sculpting new forms by combining materials in surprising ways. This fuelled his love of innovating, however, like with other areas of life he would sometimes become disheartened or bored with an idea and not finish a project. So many of his sculptures remained half-finished, lingering and just waiting for touches of the unusual when he found just the inspiration he was looking for. Bethanor always had a deep feeling of what he was hoping to emerge through his artwork and if he didn't find quite the right material or shade of colour to represent it then he would become frustrated and set the piece to one side until he stumbled on just the right thing. This made him quite temperamental. He loved to add some provocation to his works too, like a philosopher and a questioner of all things. Why would we always choose to do things in the same way when we can discover more and better ways? he would say to people.

He took out several of the pieces he had started and looked at each one of them despondently. In his mind, each one was missing something. He didn't feel proud of them so he couldn't possibly imagine presenting them at his rite of passage in three weeks time.

"What would people think?" he mused. No, he needed something "cutting edge", something that would "wow" everyone with its brilliance, with its audacity, its ingenuity.

He sat down again, staring at each one of them as if hoping the answer would just appear. It didn't. He felt a distinct lack of inspiration and he began to imagine everyone looking at his innovation with disappointment. His mind raced. His friends Inalia and Kalto would be there too. What if they'd managed to create something much better than him? That wouldn't do at all. Bethanor felt overwhelmed with pressure he was placing on himself.

He opened his media board and scanned the images and descriptions of components with a vague sense of resignation. Everything just looked so has-been to him. If he wanted his sculpture to come to life, it needed to literally give out light. Not like a lightbulb but something more subtle than that. Something, well, revolutionary.... !

Time passed as he flipped through image after image feeling more and more despondent. Then there it was.

The sculpture sat like a vision in the middle of his screen. It glowed but quite strangely, like nothing he had seen before. It almost seemed to radiate a sort of indescribable violet hue. Bethanor was captivated. How did it work? He scanned through various molecules one by one in his mind.

"No, it can't be that," he thought "it wouldn't combine. Nor that. Not the right colour, unless it came from a special fusion process...."

He was confused. He paused for a moment to calm his over-excited mind. He suddenly felt sure that he needed to know how to replicate that effect for his sculpture. This was it! As he plunged into the description of the innovation, there were very few useful details to understand the origin of the violet hue but a name appeared boldly at the bottom of the screen *"Eldregin Viador."*

"That old recluse artist," thought Bethanor "Interesting. Is he even still alive?"

He turned one of his sculptures round and round in front of him. This one would be worthy of being presented if it had that sort of violet radiating from it. The idea was so very appealing that Bethanor decided that the only way forward to achieving his dream was to seek out the old hermit himself and ask him how he'd done it. His locator said that Eldregin was even living fairly close to Bethanor's home.

"Great," he thought, "Let's do it!"

The path that led up to Eldregin's home was overgrown with a permaculture mix that was so invasive that it was almost creating its own ecosystem. It clearly hadn't been tended for a while. Bethanor pushed aside trailing tomato and bean plants that were blocking the way ahead and every so often a bee would appear through the vegetation as if to check the identity of this stranger who was wading through their generous supply of sunflowers and roses. As he progressed, his heart began to beat faster and his hands became moist with apprehension. Then through a gap in the foliage, a door appeared imposingly. A massive, heavy metallic structure bearing symbols and inscriptions in a language that Bethanor did not recognise. Just as he was bending closer to inspect the unusual emblems, a panel descended in front of him from nowhere and a holographic face appeared, analysing Bethanor curiously from head to toe.

"What are you doing here?" It asked him aggressively.

Bethanor felt nervous but straightened himself so that he wouldn't appear intimidated. The face paused, its scrutinising frown waiting for his response.

"I'm very interested in your violet sculpture Mr Viador. I don't wish to disturb your work, but I would like to ask you just a few questions if I may?"

"Everyone is interested, curious, meddling!" The face replied. "I can't help you," it bellowed and the hologram disappeared.

Bethanor was left feeling cut short. He wanted to explain the importance of his visit.

"Maybe I can help you with something in return?" Bethanor called out, not quite sure in what direction or who he should be addressing. There was no reply. He stood in the silence for a moment, and another, and another. The bees were beginning to become more frustrated by his presence, as if they could sense that he wasn't welcome. They buzzed excitedly around his head.

He stayed for a moment, looking around at the strange mix of vegetation, when a ray of sun illuminated a section of the garden that was just a few metres in front of him. In the centre of the enclosure, he saw a violet hue rise up almost majestically towards the sky. As he approached, making sure that the holographic face was nowhere to be seen, Bethanor noticed that the light was coming from crystals which had been partially implanted into the earth. They were arranged in the form of a diamond and yet the light that was refracting off each of them created a pentagon in the air above them. Bethanor smiled widely and bent down to study them further.

"What are you doing here?" asked a shaky voice behind

him. "I asked you to leave. Do you have no manners?"

Bethanor jumped with surprise and then steadied himself. "I came to ask you how you created the light effect on your work of art '*The Genesys*'," replied Bethanor.

"I see you have found what you were looking for then," replied the elderly artist looking down on Bethanor as he stooped over the living sculpture.

He was dressed ruggedly as if he had just rolled out of bed a few moments earlier. His beard was salt and pepper grey and his eyes, although somewhat sleepy were a lucid, steely grey. They looked intently at Bethanor.

"It's amazing!" enthused Bethanor not even looking at his host. "What is it? It's like nothing I've seen before."

It was obvious that Bethanor had forgotten his apprehension at being in an unwelcoming place. His face beamed with the excitement of his new discovery and his eyes were wide with expectation to understand more.

The artist covered himself more fully with a brown cape, wrapping it tightly across his frail torso. Then he bent forward and lowered himself slowly towards the ground until he was sitting next to Bethanor, only to find himself also gazing adoringly at the work of art.

"Well, if I tell you then you have to promise to keep the

secret," sparkled the artist laughing to himself. Bethanor smiled again widely and nodded in agreement.

"Let's say I was quite a rebel when I was young," started the artist still laughing quietly to himself with nostalgia. "It's called Violet Enigma, fascinating isn't it?". "I came across it for the first time during a visit to New Earth that I made with some adventurous friends many moons ago."

"You've been to New Earth?" Bethanor asked suddenly taken aback.

"Oh my, yes!" replied the artist, "several times in fact. Wouldn't recommend it though, dirty, desolate place. Easy to get lost or injured there. But then I did a lot of things as a Younger, without really thinking them through."

"That time, we took the wrong path and it was as if I was led to it. There it was, its colour just beaming out from the cliff side in front of us. I remember being mesmerised by its beauty. We sat for almost an hour just trying to analyse what it was. Most of its molecules weren't in the register. We brought some back with us and it's been here ever since! I used some in *The Genesys* as you saw but never did divulge where the violet reflection came from. People asked me of course but since it's a forbidden material, not part of the Molecular Register, I just kept a low profile. So much so that I ended up becoming quite a recluse. Hiding it really became a burden to me in my life. It looks nice in the garden though doesn't it?"

Bethanor realised at that moment that his plan for using it in his project was starting to look rather pessimistic. Indeed, the jury would know instantly if he used a material that was forbidden. His heart sank.

"I was hoping to know what it was so that I could incorporate it into the presentation for my rite of passage," he announced glumly.

The artist looked knowingly at him. "I couldn't possibly give you any. It will cause you more trouble than benefit. I think you understand that don't you?" He said gently.

"Yes, I see that now," replied Bethanor although wishing the situation could be somewhat different.

Eldregin tried to comfort his young visitor. "I'm sure you will find just the right thing for your project! Life has a way of arranging these things," he said with enthusiasm.

Bethanor thanked the artist as warmly as he could given the circumstances and stood up to leave.

"You know, people don't come here often, but you can come whenever you like to look at it if it inspires you. It always brings me so much joy. It's very soothing to the soul. I hope it helps you too," said the old man, smiling generously. Quite a stark contrast to the strict holographic face that had first appeared to speak to him.

Bethanor smiled gratefully, touched five fingers with the artist, as is the tradition in Reviathan to say hello or goodbye, and was soon on his way.

The walk seemed endless as he imagined once again his deception in front of the Committee. As Bethanor arrived back home his grandfather was waiting for him.

"Your mother was looking for you," he said gently and inquisitively to his grandson. He had a kindly face marked with many years of hard-earned wisdom, but there was still a glint of youth in his eyes that surrounded him with almost a magical aura.

Bethanor entered the compound by his grandfather's side. They sat down together in the connection room. Orothan, Bethanor's grandfather had made tea and prepared fruit freshly picked from the home's permaculture nourishment box.

"How is your project?" Asked Orothan gently.

"I'm not happy with it yet," said Bethanor sadly but honestly, "it's lacking a special something."

"Hmmm, I see," said his Grandfather nodding "Well, I

trust you will find just the right special something and when I say that, I mean that special something that makes you proud of who you are and what you share with everyone. Every presentation is unique."

He paused for a moment. "Bethanor," he said calmly "The important thing is that you understand how you fit into the greater whole of our community. The rite of passage is a moment to demonstrate your ability to create in a way which will raise the well-being of all. It is not for personal glory or an opportunity for doing anything that is reckless or may impact others negatively. This is why we only use materials that have been rigorously tested and only then incorporated into the Molecular Register, available for everyone. You also remember that as Sparks, we live by our commitment to never deform or destroy anything that is living as part of our compositions, although you may of course incorporate it into your project without changing its nature. To alter its composition would be imposing our will on another living thing. We must maintain this harmony with life and with all other living things. The environmental cataclysm showed us what happens when we do not follow these very simple principles."

Bethanor didn't say anything. A brightly coloured beetle flew down towards the table, circling the fruit plate with enthusiasm. He swiped the air in its passage gently to turn its trajectory but it seemed rather intent on discovering the source of the sweet smell that had filled the air.

"Just remember please that we are all proud of you. We have watched you create many innovations already. You have no need to prove yourself to us or to anyone else. This is a step towards fully joining the community. They are there to welcome you."

"I know Grandfather," said Bethanor quietly "I want to be proud of myself too and I don't feel it at the moment."

"Then continue to follow your heart," replied Orothan, "It will lead you in the right direction to find what you are looking for. Trust yourself."

"Why did the environmental cataclysm happen in your opinion?" Bethanor asked curiously but also trying to change the subject.

"Many refer to the period just prior to the deluge of environmental catastrophes as the 'Ostrich period'. The human population at the time knew of the impact that they were having on the Earth and the increasing risks that they were taking through not living in balance with nature, but they chose to ignore the warnings. Their creations were ingenious, intelligent but superfluous and costly in terms of using natural resources. They were disconnected from actually seeing the damage by living in concentrated settlements called cities so to many of them it did not exist. They carried on an existence which was not organised around sharing and community."

"Of course they didn't have the gifts that we have developed either so they could not compose their tools and gadgets without creating negative by-products and using lots of fossil energy from the Earth's reserves. They made their gadgets in huge polluting factories and grew their food in enormous agricultural warehouses that deprived the earth of the nutrients that it needs to regenerate. That's why the Seasons Tribe take so much care to nurture the permaculture boxes and sectors. We cannot afford to deplete what remains and we really have no need to."

"So why are we still deciding on the rules that we use to create? Why can't we be trusted if we have learnt from our mistakes?" asked Bethanor.

"You have never liked restrictions Bethanor, ever since you were small... the important thing is not to look at them as prohibitive rules but as a framework to allow us to co-create in a positive way together."

Bethanor shifted uncomfortably in his seat as his Grandfather attended to the beetle who had found its way onto a succulent piece of mango whilst they had been distracted.

"Perhaps I should ask Kalto and Inalia what they are preparing?" he announced a little more optimistically. He thanked his Grandfather and they peacefully touched five fingers together.

"This calls for a brainstorming session with my closest friends Inalia and Kalto," Bethanor thought to himself. The three had been friends since as far as Bethanor could remember. The contact between them always generated sparks of insight. Like him, they loved to not only daydream about possibilities but use their innovative capabilities to turn these into reality. They spent many an afternoon reinventing the world as they knew it.

After twisting a message onto his Messagepad, he let it disperse into the ether to find its way to Inalia and Kalto.

"Meeting in 10 minutes at the hub?"

Chapter Two

The Hideout

The group met frequently at a hideout which they had set up strategically, to the left of Inalia's house. It was particularly well-placed for sourcing strong energies coming up through Reviathan's grid and also diverted from the nearby lush gardens of Melathon. Here plants of all kinds were cultivated by the Seasons Tribe with a view to propagating them to different settlements who needed more ecological diversity.

The room was thick with objects of all kinds, charts with directions, calculations and ancient wisdom. There was a hologram of Merlin on the far wall which scintillated a silver glow. The Sparks Tribe came from a mix of ancient Nordic tribes which extended back to at least the era of Merlin the Magician. Genetically they had always had the dormant capacity to shift and combust elements, Merlin was just a precursor.

Merlin had been misunderstood by the myths that surrounded him. He developed the same gifts as the Sparks Tribespeople many moons ago. Whilst his combustions were particularly powerful, colourful and magical, (he was after all a very colourful personality), he was careful to only do good with his creations. The stories of magic only surrounded him because of a lack of understanding at the time about how the fusion process works. Our friends admired his pioneering spirit so his presence was a constant inspiration to them.

"So what's up *Ena*?" said Kalto in a wild show of curiosity. "What you creating through now?"

Inalia was waiting intently to hear. The three loved adventures and any opportunity to satisfy their endless curiosity was like music and milkshake to their hearts.

"Still trying to find that special ingredient for my project," said Bethanor "How's it going for you guys?"

"Perfectly swimmingly," said Inalia with a big smile "I've been working on it for months. I think you'll like it! I'm calling it an Authority Regulator. When someone speaks too loudly or for too long, it beeps so it alerts everyone to move on. I made it in bright pink so you can't miss it. No more boring long lectures!"

"I designed a spoon that sings to a kid as it eats so it doesn't fall asleep in its food," announced Kalto proudly. "It's almost ready, I just need to work out how to make sure the kid doesn't get up and dance instead!" he laughed.

"What are you working on?" Inalia asked looking directly at Bethanor.

"I guess it's a sort of living sculpture," said Bethanor reticently. "It welcomes people home and gives them a rundown on what happened while they were out, only it's very plain at the moment. If I could find something to enhance the composition of the moulding material it would be perfect," sighed Bethanor, his eyes scanning the room for a solution.

"Listen," said Inalia changing the subject "I'm glad that you called everyone together. You know that the build-up of the toxic gases in the Aurora Belt of our atmosphere is getting larger right? If it keeps going at this rate, they say that it's going to surpass the level of acceptable breathability within the next year because it's dispersing dangerous particles into our atmosphere. They think that it's coming from New Earth, from the damage that was done during the environmental cataclysm. I've been thinking a lot about the problem recently and I think we should contribute to the search for a solution once we're through our rite of passage. What do you think? It would be our first mission!"

"The Spark research teams have been studying the problem for some time now. Perhaps it calls for a more radical response?" said Kalto, his eyes sparkling with ideas.

"My mother says that the special innovation teams have been working on this problem for two years now. They keep trying to dissipate the gases so they're not so concentrated. Whatever they're beaming up there isn't having the impact they'd hoped for," said Bethanor.

"My father said that they are missing a primary element but they're not sure from which molecular base it could be sourced from," added Kalto.

"Exactly, that's why we're going to find it!" enthused Inalia. "It has to be out there somewhere. Nature doesn't make things unbalanced. Sparks say that for there to be harmony in the universe there is always an equal and opposite energy, everything has its place. Perhaps if we understand the current composition then we can understand what type of molecules are missing."

"We can map it with the energetic patterns of other star systems to at least determine where the missing molecules come from even if we're not allowed to use them? If they've looked at all the molecules here then perhaps it comes from somewhere else?" replied Bethanor springing back into his adventurer role.

"There's the Research Committee meeting in two weeks' time and I will have a chance to share my ideas....or rather *our* ideas if we work on something together." Inalia announced.

"Great idea! If we let our imagination really go we might just find a solution that was both harmonious and fun to create?" said Kalto in another encouraging burst of excitement. "All of the current research can be accessed on the Alpha Light Network so that anyone can propose ideas or solutions. We can tap into it from here."

As Inalia shifted into action mode, the interactive panel came down from the ceiling and the roof hatch opened to let light flood into the centre of the room. A hologram of the central network appeared in four dimensions. The light-powered communication system vibrated at a very high frequency, allowing precise visibility in line with the human eye's ability to absorb a maximum number of images and with a resolution that did not strain its healthy functioning, unlike the old screen systems. Inalia's father had been involved in developing the innovation used to activate the hologram of the communication system so she was particularly proud of his achievement and it reminded her every time she used it. This was an example of a technological innovation that helped to support and lift humanity, especially since its components were renewable and ecological. Inalia's mother reminded her regularly that it was important to think of the impact of any innovations on the life quality of future generations. Not taking this into account was a significant reason for the environmental cataclysm so everyone had learnt the lesson the hard way.

Some types of 3D printing had been banned for this reason. Instead of physically producing some items, they are available in holographic form, giving the impression they physically exist when in fact it is only a very clever use of light and illusion that makes the observer think that the object is actually there. People worry little about actually owning things. Most of the Tribespeople move between the settlements for long periods of time in order to carry out their activities. Because of this, they prefer to stay light rather than transporting cumbersome objects with them.

What Inalia loved most about this way of life was the possibility to change the decoration of her bedroom as often as she wanted. She could just reprogram her holographic viewer and it would change the colour of the walls and change the lighting into dazzling rainbow colours when she wanted something more fun, to a gentler pale green when she felt the need for some calm, or to exploding gold sparkles when she was feeling like a diva. The options were endless. Who needs to own pictures, sculptures and other objects when it is purely for display? A Reviathan bedroom now contains a very comfortable, ergonomic and mobile mattress to sleep on, a place to store clothes and natural cosmetics plus some personal sentimental objects. As for the rest, people realised that it was far more liberating to be able to live flexibly and not be psychologically over-burdened by collecting things that did not serve their day to day needs. It was also a great way to live in harmony with our changing feelings and not over exploit the Earth's resources.

The communication system revolved slowly to show red points of all of the possible points of entry into the network. Inalia reached in and pulled one of the red points towards her. As she did so it expanded into a hologram of a different sector, the famous research and development segment of the Alpha Light Network. This is where all of the Spark Tribe's research data is kept. She zoomed on a segment and asked for the "Aurora gases composition" data. Again the system expanded in a mushroom-like way to display many visual representations of the current research along with the corresponding mathematical representations. Our three dived intently into the wealth of knowledge that the system made available to them. They turned it in varying axes and delved into intriguing sections in more depth. They spent quite a few hours in reflection and discussion about what they had found, leaving light markers to find their way back to interesting references and links.

It was starting to turn dark, they could see pinks and yellows becoming more prominent through the portal in the ceiling. Our friends exchanged a final burst of ideas and then each prepared themselves to head in the direction of home, parting ways by pressing their five fingertips together with a deep respectful gaze, full of affection. Contact is important to Sparks. Taking time to look at one another as you meet and then part from one another says "*I see you*" and the contact fulfils a kinaesthetic need for connection. Their shadows weaved slowly through the old streets away from the hideout until they were out of sight.

As Bethanor approached home, he noticed that there was an animated discussion happening in the upstairs study.

"Why would this be an option?" his mother was saying. She was also discussing the urgent need for a solution for the Aurora Belt with Bethanor's grandfather, Orothan.

Bethanor spent a restless night integrating all of the information that he had gained from the Alpha Light Network. A Spark processes any data into his or her system as a reference that can be called upon at any moment. It's like uploading files into his mind that need to be organized logically and understood deeply in order to be able to draw on them at any appropriate moment. The three had scanned so much data that initially it made no sense to Bethanor and felt almost overwhelming but his capacity to store references was particularly wide so it was just a question of patience before everything would find its appropriate position. Sparks believe that everything has a perfect place in this grid of natural references in order for harmony to reign in nature. At 4 a.m. the data integration was complete and Bethanor felt a wave of calm come over him. He could now start to analyse the linkages between the new elements but that would be an activity for later that day. His eyes were heavy and sleep found him easily.

When he rose, the house was already empty. His parents had long since left to engage in their respective activities for the day, leaving a holographic care message for him as they did so frequently. Being the creative types, this time it was of a dancing and laughing hyena. Just so he could see what one looked like since there were no more of them in existence since the environmental cataclysm. His eyes sparkled with playful inspiration. Yes, today would be a whole new phase of the adventure. Back to the hideout to meet with his crew.

Inalia and Kalto were already there, scanning over the connections between elements, looking for logical patterns. "What might the research teams not have looked for?" thought Kalto, "No point in looking at the obvious, they must have done that so many times!"

"Hey guys," said Bethanor half-sleepily as he stepped through the entrance. As he approached his friends he took a half-eaten bar of chocolate from his pocket and fused it with some breakfast buns that he noticed Inalia had kindly brought with her. He thankfully munched on the resulting gourmandise. "Did you notice anything yet?" he questioned.

"We're scanning the Algorn sector of the data banks for areas that have been underestimated or excluded from further analysis," said Inalia. "We figured that the answer has to be there somewhere since the teams keep going round in circles."

"What's interesting is that they've investigated some elements but there's no data on their composition. We hit a dead end," added Kalto "The question is why would that be?"

"Indeed," agreed Bethanor "What are those elements even, I've never heard of them before?"

"They're not from here that's for sure," continued Kalto "Maybe that's why their data isn't available?'

Bethanor smiled "So we need to find out for ourselves!"

The smell of adventure filled the room and his two companions were quickly infused with the headiness of potential discovery. "Can you see anywhere where they are still trading in those elements?" he added.

"No nothing," said Inalia "It's just a blank. What now?"

"What if we go to sector four, the Eastern Suburbs?" said Bethanor, his voice becoming lower and his breathing more superficial.

The friends exchanged knowing glances. Sector Four was off limits to Youngers.

"At least they might be able to tell us something," Bethanor concluded.
"Anyone against the idea?" asked Kalto.
The room fell silent.
"Ok then," Inalia concluded "Let's do it!"

Chapter Three

Sector Four

As our team of adventurers made their way along the inner corridors of the lower arcades to Sector Four they took turns in playing the role of look-out. Sector Four was the area which spread from the back of the Eastern suburbs and cut into the hillside that extended towards access to the mainland of New Earth.

The Sparks who lived here were well known to be a mix of both researchers - looking for innovations to re-nourish the Earth post-ecolological cataclysm - and recluses, those who refused to abide by the co-creation laws of the collective Sparks community. Their activities were traced in order to avoid the appearance of innovations which could destabilise the harmony of Reviathan. Any major energy shifts were monitored by radar. And whilst people were free to come and go, it was an area where clearly our three were not permitted by their families to enter.

As they approached the inner courtyard, they watched intently as people went about their business. The difference between the researchers and recluses became more and more distinctive. Clearly the recluses had no interest in their presence whatsoever, whereas they frequently encountered the glances of researchers surprised to see Youngers in this remote outpost.

They weaved in and out amongst the stands of merchants selling potato waffle breakfasts to a diverse mix of people chatting animatedly. Since Sparks were such a social tribe with a need for contact, they had developed the practice of meeting to exchange ideas and new data first thing every morning. This ritual gave them a great sense of grounding for the day before continuing onto their own personal activities, whether in deep analysis and integration of new elements, or in creating something new. They would talk about their new discoveries of compositions and fusions with such enthusiasm that a small crowd would gather wherever an innovation was beginning to emerge in order to feed their curiosity with questions and data downloads. This is how co-creation became spontaneous and the end result would often be much more significant than the initial person's discovery or idea. To watch the process was fascinating.

Inalia, Bethanor and Kalto watched transfixed as a wave of interconnected moments of realisation swept across the small gathering of Sparks at one the breakfast stands on the far side of the square. It was almost like one synchronicity after another. You could sense and see the connections and realizations that were being made even without hearing the details of the innovation itself. The whole area would light up with inspiration and pass like small bulbs in a network from one person to another.

"This is a real hive of creativity," thought Bethanor

"Natural, effervescent, unrestricted."

How he wished to be a part of it. To be accepted as one of those people in the middle of the group, sparking thought-provoking discoveries and emerging the next social revolution!

Their hesitation and fascination did not go unnoticed to a man standing about three meters to their right. His cape was swept unkemptly across his shoulder and attached to his left side by a large emblem. A knowing, rebellious grin crept across his face as he watched the young team of explorers in front of him. Kalto noticed the man's gaze through the corner of his eye and nudged his friends. He neither looked like a researcher nor a recluse, although it was obvious from his attitude that he had been living here for some time. The figure remained motionless, only his eyes were scrutinising the new visitors with a superficial sense of having seen it all before. His intense, steely grey eyes, weather-worn face and unkempt beard made him seem rather intimidating, despite the fact that he was clearly amused by their presence. Moments later he was approaching them with a nonchalant yet self-assured stride.

"And you are?" he asked with authentic curiosity. Whilst at the same time not expecting to hear the whole true story, given the visitors adventure into these unauthorised zones.

"Em…Inalia, Kalto and Bethanor," Inalia presented in a firm yet clearly nervous fashion.

"I see," replied the stranger sceptically "What brings you to Sector Four? I am Castedon and this hive of creativity is my home. Can you feel the vitality of its life force?" he added.

The three stood stationary for an instant and then Kalto couldn't contain his enthusiasm any longer. "Yeah it's quite something isn't it!"

This made Castedon even prouder and he laughed loudly.

"Come with me, I will show you more since you're here," and he beckoned them towards the inner corridors that were leading off to the back of the square, right past where the group of Sparks were integrating the last animated discussion.

"Don't worry you're safe," he added. "'*Invenire casus victoria*' we must first adventure to find victory" he winked.

The four shadows made their way along the passage which led towards the gateway to New Earth. It smelt distinctly musty from old moisture which had seeped in and a hearty mix of moss and toadstools were proliferating up the sides of the stone walls. As they neared the light at the end of the passageway, the bustle of people haggling grew louder. Inalia felt her stomach turn somer-saults in anticipation.

A number of merchants on this side of the passageway were emerged in deep conversation with potential clients, whilst others called out to the passing group to approach.

"What are they selling?" asked Inalia.

"Old Earth remnants that have been extracted from many parts of the land and de-radiated, along with other ele-ments that they have come upon through an untracked source. You can find pretty much anything here," said Castedon.

Bethanor's world suddenly felt lit with possibility and he started to hang towards the back of the group to listen to the merchant's conversations. He could see them twisting and manipulating energies as they spoke, explaining uses and properties of their various wares.

"You go ahead," he called to the group, "You can meet me back here. I just want to explore for a while." Bethanor was thinking of his project. Maybe this time he would find that magical ingredient he was looking for, and then of course there was the research for the Aurora Belt. Perhaps something would come up for that too?

Castedon shrugged his shoulders. "Sure be my guest," he

launched "Don't buy anything I wouldn't!" he added with a short burst of amusement.

"Who are you?" asked Inalia as they continued on along the path towards the gateway. The vegetation once again started to thicken and the noise slowly dispersed into the background.

"An old hound," replied Castedon. "I have been exploring here for many moons and I see the thirst for discovery and pure creativity in your eyes. I was like you once. The Committees don't fully respect the savage nature of unbridled creativity. They want to box and restrict what we do. Here we are free to carry out our investigations in peace."

"I heard that the recluses here were reckless," added Inalia cautiously.

"That is what they would have you believe," said Castedon "So that the Committee's frameworks are respected. The most important things are the intentions that you carry when creating. If you listen for what wants to emerge through you and stay focused within your heart space then you will not create destruction. Most recluses here are rebels who believe that it is our freedom to explore and create. They do not want to be told how that should happen. That feels too engineered to us."

"How do you ensure that you stay in your heart space?"

asked Kalto.

"They did not teach you that yet?" Castedon turned, surprised. "We will pause here for a moment then," he continued.

They stopped in their tracks and took a moment to view their surroundings which were relatively wild. This part of Reviathan was almost unspoilt. The lush greenery that lined the pathway was thick with the same rich, fertile possibility. Plants and flowers of many kinds twisted around whatever rock or branch it could find closest. It was an intricate weaving of colours and forms that displayed a harmony of deep greens, pierced here and there by vibrant colours of pinks, oranges and purples. The air was heavy with the smell of jasmin and tropical hibiscus. Through some openings in this immense wall of vegetation, they could hear that the sea was crashing against some low-lying rocks as it strongly broke on the shore. Through that gap, there was nothing as far as eye could see. It felt like they could be at the end of Reviathan with only miles of waves, tossing and oscillating over and over with little else to do. In a small clearing to the left of the pathway, Castedon beckoned everyone to sit quietly.

"I invite you to settle down in the grass as often as you can and feel the ground below you," said Castedon gently. "Close your eyes and notice your breath gently flowing in and out of your nostrils. As you breath in for five, and out for five, your system slows into a peaceful state of tranquility as your brain tells the body that it no longer needs to be alert. You are safe in this present moment, no need to be thinking about anything which brings fear. Keep breathing gently and focusing your attention on the air that is coming in and then out. When we do this, our mind slows because we cannot think and feel at the same time. Slowly, as you calm your body and open your energy field to the nature around you, you will start to feel yourself as part of something bigger than yourself. You connect to the universal network of energy, Reviathan. Feel its expansiveness, its flow and its acceptance of all things. Here we can resource for a moment and allow ourselves to receive any feeling or inspiration that may come to us."

The three remained motionless for several moments. The wind blew past, wrapping them nurturingly for a brief moment in its passage.

"Listen to your heart beating, then think of someone or a place that you love and focus on the area around your heart, this is your heart space. Feel the warm connection between you and the person you care about. We can sense ourselves as part of something bigger than just our body. Listen now to the sounds of all things around you and feel yourself in harmony with that, as one small but vital, magical part of that. In doing this you can feel a sense of peace come over you. Just sit, just be, nothing more."

Inalia felt a strange sense of knowing come over her, like she had done this before or felt this sense of calm somewhere. It felt pleasant and relaxing, as if in some way she didn't need anything else right at that moment.

"This is how you get into your heart space," said Castedon, "When you can move into this sense of peacefulness at any moment, through practice, then you are living in your heart space. The most authentic kinds of creativity come from the heart. The heart is courage, it doesn't know fear, only the mind does. The heart has an incredible sense of where it needs to go if we listen closely to our inner voices during these moments. We just need to trust it to let it help us to create."

As he concentrated on his heart space and thought of his faithful dog *Rockstar*, Kalto felt a sense of basking in rays of light, as part of a bigger matrix of energy within which he could distinguish the different vibrations. He almost felt as if his body did not exist, as if it was disintegrating away. Sparks could of course decompose any object but it had never occurred to him that he could do that even to himself.

"So weird!" he thought. It was as if he was understanding, through feeling, exactly how his bones, blood, tissues and muscles had all been generated in the first place. He felt his entire energy system vibrating gently as part of the infinite universal energy network. "Wow that's quite something," he mused to himself.

He felt like just a small particle which is part of an amazing interdependent dance of elements. In that moment nothing else either existed or impacted his sense of well-being. In his mind's eye he could see the energy waves moving like a soft haze.

Our three sat in peace, just feeling the inner stillness for several moments more and as they opened their eyes they felt full of energy and ready once again to explore.

Meanwhile Bethanor, to the contrary, was haggling animatedly with a merchant. He was also busy gleaning as much information as his mind could absorb as he was listening to three different conversations around him. All three were discussing different basic elements that he had never in his life heard of. This place was treasure trove of experiments he thought. Bethanor's idea of nirvana!

The material he was attempting to purchase was a green, molecular, half metal, half crystal composition. It was clear to him that the fusion gained from these two main elements had not occurred within the confines of Reviathan and was perhaps not even of this world. The merchant was being evasive with his replies to Bethanor's questions so it must contain an illegal molecule.

"Why would that be?" pondered Bethanor. "Was it formed using non-validated creative practices or perhaps it even contained illegal, unstable molecules?"

The merchant could easily see the enthusiasm that Bethanor was trying to hide so it was proving difficult to reduce the price.

"Ok," said Bethanor, "I will take it for 3000 Reviathan tokens, but only if you tell me its origin."

"This I will do," said the merchant puffing out his chest in pride, but I cannot say how I came about owning it."

"No need," reassured Bethanor and so the deal was struck.

The merchant's features softened with relief at having come to an agreement. His face was weathered from a hard life of commerce but his eyes were not harsh and they looked at Bethanor as if trying to understand his motivations. He opened his cape, feeling more at ease with his new acquaintance and smiled, revealing a dragon tattoo on his front-right tooth. Bethanor had thought it was a stain. The man's hands were gnarled and covered with rings of many origins. His long, black hair was plaited in a braid to one side containing a single silver thread with a symbol appearing at the end. Never in his life had Bethanor seen such an oddly, eccentric character. The energy between them became one of mutual respect, despite a little suspicion that had surrounded the trade.

Bethanor stood motionless for a moment, integrating all of the new data that he had just taken in from his environment. He wanted to concentrate to be able to focus in on this new ingredient without any confusion. How was he going to integrate it into his project without anyone being able to tell where it came from? Perhaps he could just use part of it?

He searched his inner pocket to reveal three crisp Reviathon notes and handed them to the smiling merchant who quickly folded them away under his cloak. He then poised himself and looked deeply at Bethanor with his fiercely purple gaze.

"What you are looking for has found you my adventurer. This day you have come to feel the vibration of Chomavelia. This is a highly volatile fusion which contains the essence of all colour, captured through the crystalline properties of clear quartz and Zethan which comes from Stargate Melanon. The metallic components, Helianteel and Stroic, were extracted from the mines of Melor during a ceremony of remembrance. They are combined to provide both the properties of conductivity and strength. You will not find another element like it in Reviathan, I guarantee it. I had to import it specially," said the merchant with a wink and a glint in his eye.

"I advise you to take great care of it," he continued

"Which means do not leave it exposed to direct sunlight as it refracts powerfully. I'm not even sure what might happen but certainly its volatility may make it like a fire-cracker. May I ask how you are going to use it?"

"I have no idea yet," said Bethanor, "But my intuition is telling me that it is a composition close to this form that I need so I'm going to decompose it further to investigate."

"Sure, be my guest!" said the merchant laughing to him-self "Enjoy! I wish you well my friend" he concluded.

Bethanor touched five fingers with the merchant and smiled.

He loitered for a while in the area listening for more tips from passers by. Methods of fusion that he'd never even imagined and laws of combination that seemed wildly unpredictable but whose outcome he would definitely be intrigued to understand. Here he was in the midst of a hub of amazing knowledge and possibility. It felt quite surreal yet at the same time deeply engaging. He was so inspired that he wasn't convinced that he ever wanted to leave. But then he quickly startled himself out of his daydream, reminding himself of the fact that he wasn't supposed to be there in the first place. Carefully wrap-ping his new, intriguing purchase within one of the inner repositories of his jacket, he set off along the pathway to catch up with the others. He was feeling quite proud of himself.

He could see Kalto, Inalia and Castedon in the distance making their way through the vegetation towards what must be the frontier with New Earth. With just a hint of acceleration he would be with them in no time.

From the boundary of Sector Four, the Eastern Suburbs, they looked out towards New Earth and the adventure that awaited them. Reviathan with its nurturing greenery beckoned them to stay. The immense devastation would be a stark contrast with the lushness of Reviathan, shocking in its reality so they prepared themselves psychologically. The friends were not even born when the environmental cataclysm had occurred. They had pictured the vast desolation in their fertile imaginations but only now that they saw it with their own eyes could they comprehend the extent of the damage to New Earth. Dryness for as far as the eye can see. A greyish sandstorm was whipping across the crevasses at the frontier, bringing with it what little life remained in the form of weeds and old branches.

As they stood at the edge, they noticed the outline of a figure appear through the sandstorm in the distance. It approached cautiously, continuously resetting its balance, its cape wrapped firmly around it's body which bent slightly over in order to avoid the aggressively swirling grains of sand. It affronted the wind with a courageous determination. The hood of the cape covered

the figure's features as it neared the group. Almost as if
there was an invisible wall, there was suddenly no more
wind past the edge of New Earth. As our mysterious figure stepped over the boundary of Reviathan there was a
resounding gasp for air, followed by hoarse coughing.
The figure made an abrupt halt and slowly pulled back
his hood as he neared the group. His eyes were of a
metallic silver which glistened in the mid-morning light.
Castedon noticed that his visitors were taken aback by
the adventurer's appearance.

"Too much time exploring the mines of New Earth, your
eyes give you away every time but I'm sure you haven't
lost your sense of humour my dear friend," Castedon
called out to the stranger, opening his arms in a wide,
welcoming embrace. "I am very glad to see you once
more Ellianon," he continued. "Meet my friends
Bethanor, Inalia and Kalto."

Ellianon reached out a firm arm to receive the guests of
the Eastern suburbs, bowing his head with respect as he
always did and then reaching out to touch five fingers
with each of them.

When we have strength there is no fear in revering others. We know of our worth. It was clear from his stance
that Ellianon was an experienced adventurer with many a
story to tell no doubt. His face was marked with small
scars and his clothes were strapped all over with small
pockets for the elements he discovered during his travels

on the mainland.

Curiosity filled the conversations as our party made their way back towards the safety of Reviathan.

"Let us sit together to drink and partake in your story Ellianon," proposed Castedon.

Ellianon revealed a broad smile. He loved nothing more than to share his adventures, especially since he would spend many days on the dirt tracks without seeing any other living creature so these opportunities of reconnection and sharing were moments he deeply appreciated.

Ellianon was not a merchant but a forager. Whilst the committees did not approve of his methods of scavenging for remnants of the old Earth regime, they were particularly useful sources of information and inspiration for Reviathan's research labs.

He had journeyed out beyond the Magentan Caves to see whether the Emissary of Andenan still lived as a hermit in the nearby surroundings. He had heard of the Emissary's wish to share the ancient Nordic philosophies on the importance of *issu* (courage and tenacity), *hygge* (a feeling of well-being and cocooning) and *lagom* (the just measure, only using what we need). These were the roots of the Spark's heritage after all. Within the walls of the caves were elements of lithium and the site had been used as a sanctuary of gathering of people from all backgrounds. Because of this Ellianon hypothesised that there may well be the remains of different habitations with objects from many different horizons. The trip had taken him 38 days to arrive at the caves meeting many interesting characters from different tribes on the way. There was little ground transportation anymore since non-renewable fuel consumption had been banned and the larger "Droid Regsters" were not yet available to the masses to overfly nearby territories. The Committee considered them too dangerous. They feared that a Younger would venture across the boundary too easily and without assistance and in the harsh climate, anything could go wrong. Ellianon walked mostly and occasionally hitched a ride with passing nomads.

He met one such nomad on the outskirts of Lianville, a well-known New Earth town that is around 190 kilometers North of the Eastern Suburbs. He was watering his horses at a local oasis hub. His name was Yargen.

Nomads are mostly of Star Tribe origin. Their freedom is more precious to them than anything else and they roam the planet offering their mediation services wherever they may be needed because of conflict. The remarkable thing about Stars is their ability to time jump in order to observe events from different perspectives and therefore understand the causes of disputes. The first time he saw this happen, Ellianon watched in awe as Yargen's body continued to function whilst it was very clear that his soul had just switched timelines to arbitrate a disagreement in another dimension. As he returned to our reality, he grinned widely. There is nothing a Star likes to do more than help to resolve a dispute. After studying events for many years, they have a neutral perspective. This comes through their ability to observe all sides of an argument, they don't judge other people.

"Hello my friend," Yargen launched enthusiastically as he opened his arms widely to welcome Ellianon.

His head was shaved on one side where he had tattooed a picture of The Tree of Life, symbolising eternal life and wisdom. The friends hugged and then looked at each other with deep respect as they touched their five fingers together. Ellianon had always thought that Yargen had a sense of Spark Tribe curiosity in him. He was constantly bringing back objects from other dimensions which formed a basis for some interesting conversations between them. Matter was available in many other forms in some of the places he jumped to, so he'd catch many of them floating around. Because of this, he had to be extremely careful in bringing them back so that when they came under pressure from gravity, they would not implode or become unstable in any way.

Lianville was a very old, deserted human settlement which was arranged in a semi-circle, most likely to protect the former inhabitants from sandstorms. They most likely left over 50 years ago after having tried to fortify the walls against the encroaching environmental damage.

There were still water supplies coming from a deep underground stream so many travellers stopped here to fill their tanks and compare stories before moving on to other adventures. There was less likelihood that the water was toxic here. Sparks could of course decompose it to remove any harmful elements, but Stars don't have this capacity so Yargen was particularly happy to meet Ellianon who gladly helped him replenish his supplies.

As the friends sat together, basking in the warmth of each others delight at their reunion, Yargen shared a story from his last voyage. He had heard of two young Stars who had fallen so deeply in love that they had gone against all the sacred codes of time jumping in order to see each other again.

"The story of course intrigues me so I'm trying to find out what happened to them. It is quite amazing what we will sometimes do in the name of love, don't you think?" Yargen enthused.

He was so very neutral that he found such impulsive behaviour hard to understand. Inalia was listening intently to Ellianon's story "how romantic" she thought to herself. Yargen was a pillar of integrity. He was a widely travelled and deeply respected mediator, who had dedicated his whole life to seeking the truth and helping others to do the same. The Star Tribe have an ancient saying which came from one of their teachers, Buddha *"Three things cannot be long hidden: the sun, the moon, and the truth"* Yargen would say. Bethanor shifted uncomfortably in his chair.

As their conversation came to a close, Ellianon traded a Vestinari stone with Yargen found on the Endorian Plateau. This material was very rare in Reviathan and could be used for many types of cleansing, yet Yargen had no need for it. In other dimensions he could find it quite easily. This was yet another unusual material that Bethanor immediately became interested in hearing about.

"What is it used for?" he asked.

"Generally it's caustic," said Castedon "It disintegrates the top layer of many different materials in order to force it to regenerate. A bit like the skin. The top layer is mostly dead skin cells. When we remove them by scrubbing, the skin underneath feels soft and regrows more easily. The Vestinari does this on more robust surfaces."

"How *exactly* does it do that to other objects?" asked Bethanor, his nervous curiosity getting the better of him.

"Well, it's sort of like an organism that energetically interacts with its target by kick-starting its repair process. It can seem like it is being aggressive but if you study it carefully, it is actually very benevolent. It detects intuitively what needs to be repaired and it blankets the target, dissolving the disfunctioning top layer and subsequently transferring some of its own vital energy to it in order to regenerate."

"Wow, we should really put these everywhere on New Earth!" Inalia added to the conversation.

"Indeed we should," said Ellianon enthusiastically "There just aren't enough of them and the target still needs nutrients afterwards in order to continue to repair itself. Although they can regenerate their targets, we have yet to understand how it reproduces itself or if there is a larger source of them available somewhere."

"Can I touch it?" asked Bethanor.

"Sure," replied Ellianon "I will even sell it to you for the same price that I purchased it since I can sense your enthusiasm and I see that you are perhaps on the lookout for unusual pieces?" he laughed. "I analysed your coat and I saw the Chromavelia. Don't worry, I will not say anything. May I ask why you are collecting these things?"

"We are investigating the Aurora Belt decomposition," Kalto added, "We are looking for new avenues to explore."

"Well you are certainly looking in the right place for unexplored avenues," added Castedon laughing, "The Committee would certainly not look here, at least not officially."

"Chromavelia hey?" said Ellianon "That also has regenerative properties. Different from Vestinari, very different. More volatile, less nurturing. But you could certainly look at how the tear in the layer might be regenerated rather than simply patched up. The rumours say that the research teams are just trying as much as possible to close it at the moment."

"How do you know what they are trying to do?" asked Inalia inquisitively, "I thought you were always away exploring?"

"Let's say people keep me informed," smiled Ellianon "So I can see what they might need in the way of supplies."

"So you are interested in the question too?" Bethanor asked.

"Of course, who wouldn't be?" replied Ellianon "Apart from picking up useful samples, it's also the basis of many an animated conversation here in the Eastern Suburbs."

"What do people here think the answer is?" asked Kalto

"Oh it varies but certainly, everyone is in agreement that the solution lies outside the list of validated elements in the Molecular Register. They have been analysed and combined so many times."

"Many say that the solution to the Aurora Belt deterioration will come through the Eastern Suburbs," added Kalto.

"It can only be that way. It is a problem that needs to be addressed through pure creativity and openness to other elements from places who have already learned how to regenerate effectively without side-effects to the rest of the environment. We Sparks are still struggling with that." Ellianon continued "There are several people here carrying out independent research. They are some of the first to greet me when I return and who are most open to my discoveries. In fact they have become close friends and we discuss possibilities together. Their search is altruistic. Driven only by the wish to ensure our planet perpetuates in a sustainable and harmonious way for the next generations. I enjoy being a part of that. It gives purpose to my long journeys. We are all seekers but in many different forms."

"Do you think we can meet them?" asked Inalia "Sparks believe in diversity, creativity, spontaneity and togetherness. Co-creation is in our genes after all, it seems a shame not to exchange ideas when we are all searching for the same thing."

"Why not indeed," said Ellianon "I would be delighted to see them shortly. My journey was long. Let me clean up and I can meet you in the main square in one hour. We will see who is available."

Chapter Four

The Jade Lady

As our group arrived in the square Ellianon was already waiting for them. Propped against a bar he was talking animatedly to a lady who was wearing a rather conspicuous jade and velvet braid in her hair. Her black hair was streaked with grey. "She must have been one of the researchers that Ellianon had mentioned" thought Bethanor. He was showing some of the objects to her which were laid out carefully on the bar in front of her. She was concentrating intently on every word he said, but Bethanor could tell she was integrating new data in real time as he was speaking. "wow, so cool" thought Bethanor "no more moments of isolation to integrate new information, she's like a real time data processor, only she has arms and legs!" he laughed. He decided it was better to keep that joke to himself since they were about to meet.

"Argolia, delighted to meet you" said the lady reaching out her hand to greet each member of the group.

Close up her beauty was breathtaking, you would barely notice her age. She had a lightness about her and her features were soft. Each member of the group presented themselves, Castedon as usual bearing a large smile.

They were soon joined by two men, both researchers, as was Argolia the Jade Lady. A large circular sofa was awaiting our guests as was the custom. It was far easier to have group discussions around a circular seating arrangement and Sparks were always together discussing things. Ellianon continued on with an animated exposé of his voyage, gesticulating wildly at moments of tense adventure. Kalto was perched on the edge of his seat whist Bethanor was more concerned with the details of Ellianon's discoveries. His mind raced as he imagined the decomposition of each of the exotic materials and the vast possibilities for combining them into something new. The elements were all laid out on the low table in front of them, each one more obscure-looking than the previous. This place is phenomenal he thought, it felt refreshing to him in many ways.

What would his mother think though? "*Woah*, let's not even go there!" He thought "She would freak!"

"May I analyse it?" Bethanor asked not being able to contain his enthusiasm as Ellianon displayed a large piece of reddish-brown coloured metal to everyone.

"Are you sure you can put it back together again?" asked Ellianon cautiously.

"I'll watch," Castedon suggested "I'll be able to adjust if necessary as it's recomposed."

"Sure," Ellianon agreed and he smiled as he watched Bethanor pick up the object, lift it to his line of sight and proceed to decompose it little by little. Bethanor was concentrating hard to make certain he noted the presence of each molecule. As he did so the material disintegrated into flows of colours before everyone's eyes. All eyes in the room watched inquisitively.

"Look, did you see that?" asked the jade lady "There, the matter just shifted a frequency. Fascinating!"

The conversation turned to how Ellianon had found the elements and Kalto asked whether any of them were listed in the Molecular Register or if they were all outlaw materials? The group fell silent for a short moment.

"We work a lot here with unlisted elements," replied Castedon, "That's the whole point of being here. We believe no stone should be left unturned in our analysis, however unpopular that view may be. Breakthroughs can only be made by going beyond what we think we know to be true." Kalto nodded in understanding.

On that point, one of the researchers added "If we don't test and analyse them we cannot know for sure whether they are volatile or dangerous, it's just an assumption that we start from. This happens behind the scenes before they are officially integrated into the Molecular Register for everyone to use. Many of us have worked for years with the Committee doing these analyses before coming here to carry them out independently so we know what we are doing and use the same levels of safety. We like to work with more freedom and things are quicker around here," he smiled.

This led the group to start discussing what is acceptable or not.

"If we're totally free to create anything, couldn't that be dangerous for humanity," questioned Inalia.

"Well" said the Jade Lady "We all choose to live by the criteria of creating only what lifts rather than lowers humanity. This is of course questionable but this is why we spend so much time discussing different perspectives of potential solutions and impacts all together. It's not just a social pastime but also a fundamental way of double-checking that we always behave in accordance with our values. You need to be a bit of a rebel to think and act outside of the box, to question everything but we also do listen to the thoughts of others who are also progressive thinkers themselves. Staying heart-centred is the best way. It makes a big difference if your intention is to innovate for the benefit of others."

"So you don't think in future we might invent something again which will destroy the environment like we did in the past?" continued Inalia.

"It took us a while to realise our actions. We did not

place sufficient importance on protecting and nurturing the Earth so we turned a blind eye to destructive actions. We pillaged and manipulated nature, leaving much of her in such desolation that she started to attack herself like a cancer. As such we suffered the consequences. We are still old enough to have lived through that and so we create now with humility and care. It is important that future generations remember this terrible part of our history so that it never repeats".

The lady paused to wait for further enquiry from Inalia or anyone, with a peaceful sense of openness. Inalia could tell that she was not forcefully trying to convince but just share her experience and beliefs and this touched her.

"So I guess you don't believe in just creating anything in that case?" she asked. "Does it lift or lower humanity that is the question? I will let you decide for yourself based on what you have seen and heard here today," she said with a wide smile "You are old enough to have your own opinion and the more you cultivate trust in yourself the better."

In the background Bethanor was busy recomposing the piece of metal with as much care as a surgeon.

"Aha!" he exclaimed with delight as if he'd just found the answer to a complicated puzzle, "Done!" He said as he put it back down on the table.

Castedon nodded in agreement "perfect!" he reassured "I even timed you, 2 minutes 13 seconds!" he added laughing to himself.

The room applauded and Bethanor blushed with pride.

Inalia, Kalto and Bethanor had spent a good proportion of the day discovering the Eastern Suburbs. Much more than they were initially intending. They did not want to raise the suspicion of their parents so they thanked their hosts for sharing so much with them and wished them well, promising to return soon to continue their research.

"Call on us as you wish," offered the Jade Lady as they were leaving.

"I will even take you over to the New Earth side if you would like to see it for yourselves?" offered Ellianon and he added reassuringly "You are safe with me. I know all the paths." Their faces were lit with excitement just at the thought. They looked at one another and replied with a unanimous "Would we!"

Chapter Five

Discovering New Earth

Bethanor didn't sleep much thinking about the wild possibility of exploring New Earth. It was something he had dreamt about longingly since he was small and had found himself gazing at the large, interactive screens and holograms of how the Earth used to be at his school. "One day I'll visit there" he had wished and sure enough that day had arrived. They left their homes early in the morning so they could manage to fit in as full a day as possible, Kalto bringing with him some snacks to share. They retraced their footsteps from the previous day, memories came flooding back as they took each step along the passageway to Sector Four which was now becoming so familiar.

As the sun rose higher in the sky, our friends decided to take a rest, pausing at some rocks that were beckoning them only a few meters from the side of the pathway.

"Let's put ourselves back into our heart fields while we sit," suggested Inalia. "We can show you what to do Bethanor. Castedon showed us yesterday while you were busy with the merchants. He said it was important to create from this space to ensure that it is coming through with purity of intention."

Bethanor looked intrigued.

"That's how you can tell if what you're creating will lift or lower humanity," added Kalto.

"Sure," said Bethanor settling himself on the highest rock so he could see the way ahead.

"The point is to focus our attention on the present moment," said Inalia tapping Bethanor gently on the shoulder to get his attention. "You can only affect the future with the positive energy that you put into your life today".

Our friends sat motionless, feeling the wind once again around their shoulders, teasing them for attention. They remained in silent communion for several minutes preparing for the excursion ahead. As they opened their eyes they could not believe what they saw. There was a small creature sitting proudly soaking up the sun, and waiting inquisitively for them to notice its presence. It looked like a cross between a bird and a lizard, only without a full covering of feathers. As Inalia and Kalto looked back at it curiously, the creature showed its delight, tipping its head to one side as if inviting them to interact.

"Do you think it wants to eat some of my Hepster bar?" said Kalto reaching into his jacket pocket and rummaging around. He whipped out a golden wrapper with pride and held a piece towards the creature. It turned its face away.

"Not sure it does," said Bethanor "I guess it's not really lizard staple diet."

"But everyone loves Hepsters!" replied Kalto looking disappointed. He rolled the piece into a ball and tossed it into his mouth. The lizard-bird looked more amused by this game than by the idea of food.

"What are you doing here?" asked Inalia gently to the creature "Do you have a home?"

The lizard-bird closed its eyes and a silver-hued shimmer of light formed above its head. Slowly as our friends looked on, the energy transformed into an image of a nest perched on some rocks, high up away from the Eastern Suburbs. They could just make out the shape of Mount Kailim in the background meaning that it must be somewhere overlooking the Valley of Oron. As the image dispersed, Kalto and Bethanor exchanged 'woah' glances. This was better than the Alpha Light Network!

"Can you show us the tear in the Aurora belt?" asked Kalto

The lizard-bird once again closed its eyes and the silver hue gave way once again to clouds, then swirling atmospheric airflows until the image stopped at a haze of greys and browns. There was an upward flow of this toxic air that appeared to be escaping into another area of the Earth's protective layers. Two birds who were flying past radically changed trajectory to pass under the rust-coloured cloud formations. They had to engage substantially more effort to bypass the air currents and Inalia was worried that they might be suffocated in some way. The lizard-bird's eye blinked open and it smiled with a certain pride at its ability to respond to Kalto's request.

"Where can we find a solution to repair the tear?" asked Bethanor trying to contain his disbelief.

Once again the creature allowed the friends to see what was requested of it. The energy shifted to a desolate, dark grey zone with only rocks as far as the eye could see. There was just a small patch of trees, only one of which was standing majestically to the left. Its branches were broken in several places but its trunk was strong, perhaps as wide as as a doorway. There was a strange light around the tree, a green and magenta haze that was barely noticeable to the regular eye, but to a Spark it could not be missed. Then at the foot of the tree, they could make out the form of a blue-grey chalk-like material. From a distance, they could decipher through a process of analytic deduction that they had never seen at least two of the components before.

They looked at one another trying to ascertain if one of them had noticed anything else. Impossible. The elements were clearly not from the Molecular Register but perhaps Ellianon would know. As the image faded the lizard-bird opened its wings widely as if intending to stretch but with a snap reflex it was launching itself into the air and once again circling overhead. It dived gracefully towards New Earth as if to indicate the way and then swooped off towards the Valley of Oron.

Inalia leapt to her feet and started to pace as she integrated the information they had just received. All were deep in thought.

"Let's go," suggested Kalto "I'm sure we can find more information in the Eastern Suburbs. Ellianon will be waiting for us."

Their guides were once again waiting for them. It was fairly simple to detect the arrival of three shadows in the distance, drawing closer and closer. It was rare that other Sparks visited these parts.

"Good morning, my friends" said Ellianon raising his five fingertips to each of them in a warm greeting. "Are you ready to discover what is on the other side of our beautiful Reviathan?" he added enthusiastically, folding his cloak over his left shoulder in readiness for action.

Inalia opened an excited recount of their encounter with the lizard-bird. Ellianon listened intently. He had heard of a lizard-bird-like creature called an Enadon. The Star Tribe spoke of, and even revered their abilities to share certain truths through visions. They are part eagle, considered to be the majestic connectors of earth and sky, and part iguana lizard. It is well known that lizards have very strong instincts for survival and regeneration. No-one knew quite how they had developed their visionary capacities. It is generally considered that they must have done so in order to survive from the environmental cataclysm, just like the Reviathan tribes had developed their own abilities. Maybe, however, they were just the result of some strange experiment when people were allowed to manipulate DNA. Ellianon had seen one circling in the airs above him at least twice, but he had never been fortunate enough to actually interact with one of these unusual creatures.

"It must have taken a liking to you. Perhaps it recognised your part in wanting to restore the atmosphere to its former balanced state. I suppose it could feel that your quest was heart-centred and authentic and it wanted to help you, but it can only reply to questions through images." Ellianon paused, then concluded "At least it gives us a clue that it is possible to repair the tear in the Aurora Belt and that is encouraging."

"I've always thought it was possible," said Bethanor haughtily.

Ellianon looked over at him with a knowing smile. "Indeed we all hoped that it would be possible. I'm glad you trust your intuition so strongly. What did you see?"

"Just rocks, miles of grey rocks and just one special tree in the centre of a small group which was damaged but still standing proudly. It looked like a very old pine tree and there was a green and magenta haze around it," said Kalto

"That could be the Tree of Justice as the ancients called it," mused Ellianon. "If it is the tree I am thinking of I have seen it during my travels. I can go there but I cannot take you as the journey will be too long."

"But we still don't know what materials we are looking for there," added Inalia

"Yes but we can explore. And that is what I do best!" said Ellianon in a sprited fashion, suddenly finding his place in the emerging adventure. "Shall we go?" he added "I will take sufficient rations so that I can go there alone without delay. We can set off together and Castedon will bring you back later today once you have seen what you came to see. You cannot be away for long."

And with that Ellianon disappeared into the nearby doorway to make his final preparations.

The Jade Lady was talking in a crowd gathered at the corner of the square. She was looking inquisitively at the man opposite her. At a moment of pause she nodded and removed a large piece of yellow mineral from a bag that was slung across her shoulder. She held it aloft in front of them and turned it gently. Both of them proceeded to decompose the element, continuing to talk in an animated way as they did so. The man's eyes suddenly lit up with excitement as he realised the potential of the material. He thanked the jade lady, touched fingers with her and left with a spring in his step. Our friends approached Argolia slowly to greet her.

"What did you find?" asked Inalia curiously.

"It's from the remnants of a mineral bed in one of the Northern sectors of New Earth," said the lady "It contains a mix of sulphur and some random elements of iron ore. It's one of the materials that Ellianon brought back from his last travels. We had been discussing a difficulty in fusing the sulphur with another element that the man has been testing. I figured it might help."

"Can he get some more?" asked Inalia

"He can make the part that he needs now that he knows the composition," replied the lady with a broad smile "No need to move!"

As Ellianon reappeared shortly afterwards Inalia was still in mid flow of describing their encounter with the Enadon.

"I look forward to hearing about your adventures," enthused the Jade Lady. "It seems that you are being well guided," she added revealing another of her enigmatic smiles. With that final word, the acquaintances touched fingers and started off on the pathway out of the city and towards the border of Reviathan.

The plan was to advance only about 10 kilometres along the Northern coastline. This would take Ellianon in the right direction to arrive at the Tree of Justice a day later and it would be safer for everyone. Packs were slung to the ground, buckles tightened, scarves wrapped tightly to avoid sand entering into their clothes and hair, and masks aligned. Each member of the party removed their Regsters from their packs and fired them up, preparing for departure. The gentle whirring sound could be heard resonating across the valley. They stepped on one by one, poised and waiting to embark on the adventure. Their shadows trailing long across the low hazy sun.

"Whoa" they heard from behind them. Kalto was frantically waiving his arms in the air as he tried to mount and find his balance on the board which was hovering a little too high off the ground for him.

"Who programmed these things?" he asked "I ain't goin' nowhere far on this!" The Regster swung from side to side and circled, before coming to an abrupt stop.

"Not game," said Kalto blushing.

He found his composure and then signalled victoriously into the distance "To the discovery of New Earth, lead the way!" he called out.

Everyone laughed, smiling fondly at Kalto's tricks. This truly was an adventure and they were ready.

With the sandstorm conditions, they would need to advance slowly and stay close together. With everyone ready, the group started out keeping a streamlined order to limit the impact of the on-coming wind, Castedon closing the line behind.

As they crossed the threshold, they watched the lushness of Reviathan fall away into the distance. A light fog of heat haze came over them, rising out of the far horizon as they advanced. They had to wear full-face masks to protect their eyes not just from the microscopic grains of sand but its toxic mixture with other elements. The sea below ravaged as Inalia looked down. She felt a little dizzy and sick, the sudden increase in temperature was quite overwhelming. She stopped for a moment to acclimatise. Kalto came closer and encouraged her to breathe deeply and concentrate on the present moment to ensure she didn't panic. She took three deep breaths poising herself, then nodded that she was ready to proceed. The rest of the party advanced behind, Sparks can be amazingly quick but in the spirit of togetherness, they always move at the pace of the slowest member when in travelling in groups.

As they they set foot on New Earth the party was silent.
They paused to take in their surroundings. Through the
lightly whipping sandstorm they could make out the endless miles of barren desert. Bethanor's heart sank as he
realized the horror of how a once green and prosperous
land similar to Reviathan could have become so desolate.

"How could we not have seen this coming? I guess we
could never have imagined that this would truly come
about one day. It is unimaginable" he thought. Yet here
they were and it was almost impossible to believe the
extent of the emptiness around them, no animals, no
vegetation, just a few random, dilapidated buildings dot-
ted here and there."

As the party advanced into the open land, our friends
could not believe their eyes. They had heard of the environmental impact but to see it was quite another thing.
Parts of the land were violently cracked open, others
looked to be decomposing as the hot sun scorched what
little remained of tree trunks and vines. This had once
been a vibrant forest full of thousands of types of
species, stretching for 60,000 acres according to the his-
torical maps of the Earth. Now all that remained was
twisted, dead bark and dust. To a Spark whose whole life
is dedicated to recomposing elements to create something new, this was a devastating sight.

As they progressed, the party saw large areas of land that

were being regenerated with the Season Tribe's recognizable crystal gridding. The Seasons live in harmony with the cycle of nature so they accepted the challenge of patiently and lovingly finding a way of bringing the lands back to life. They did this through thoroughly cleaning and decontaminating the earth and then replanting buds that were transferred from Reviathan. It was a long, painstaking process which covered only a few new acres each year.

Sparks, to the contrary, reuse materials right down to the smallest molecule in order to combine them into something new. They can't repair an atom that is damaged, they just remove them from the overall composition. Because of that, as they flew past the different areas, they analysed their surroundings just to gauge whether it had the potential to regenerate or not. Were all of the elements in their surroundings really dead?

It uses a lot of vital energy to do fusion work so to our friends, who were used to solving problems of a much smaller scale, the vast desolation seemed an almost insurmountable feat for the human race to recondition. Kalto swallowed hard at the realisation. Bethanor was still feeling choked, whilst Inalia just seemed almost mesmerised. Even when they paused for a brief moment, few words were exchanged. Eyes were moist with sadness but their curiosity remained. Surely there must be a way to have more of an impact, to restore things to the way they were…? Their minds raced as they imagined so many combinations of options and this gave their hearts some sliver of hope.

Castedon looked at their shock with compassion "Human beings need hope, this is what makes us different to animals. We can create a shared vision from which anything could be possible eventually, especially to an innovator!" he said comfortingly "When all else fails, there is always hope."

As the group rounded a steep cliffside, they saw the way ahead descend into a deep ravine. The sides were lined with cragged rocks and minerals as if they had been ripped out from the depths of the Earth, its treasures exposed for all to see. This is the kind of place where Ellianon would discover new elements to bring back for investigation by the research teams. The existence of many of them was not known to early man as they were deep within the layers of magma. Forced up from the Earth's core, they were offered up for research, as if she wanted us to find the solutions to her traumas. To help rebuild her to her former glory. It was as if we were being given clues to resolving the puzzle.

They lowered their Regsters one by one, into the crevasse, maintaining the same rigorous care with each action. Ellianon stopped briefly at a deposit that was more easily accessible than the rest, lodged in the side of the ravine. He decomposed part of the rock face so he could loosen a piece of mineral that looked, as he gently lifted it out, like a violet flame was alight on its inside. It caught a ray of light through the haze and the colour dazzled, lighting up the entire cliff face. The beauty of the moment was breathtaking.

Kalto almost lost his balance again as he leaned back away from the light in surprise. "What is it?" he asked.

"It's a Violet Enigma'" replied Ellianon "Its properties are still being explored. Fascinating piece, it looks as if there are many facets of a flame inside. I like to think of it as our vital spark at the core of the crystal gleaming out. It's one of my favourites. I come here quite often to see it."

Bethanor recognised the Violet Enigma as the crystal that he had seen in Eldregin's garden. So this was the source. He felt filled with the same wonder and intrigued as to whether Ellianon was going to reveal any more of its properties.

As Inalia looked around the ravine there was a certain silence here that contrasted greatly with all the devastation that they had seen around them. Standing in a peaceful violet haze, it was as if time was standing still for them. The trauma of the environmental cataclysm was past, Earth was now waiting patiently to be soothed.

There was some life here further down the ravine, some tiny pockets of refuge from the sandstorms where some plants were starting to grow again. Ellianon carefully wrapped the Violet Enigma and secured it safely inside his pack as the party prepared to descend lower into the ravine in order to investigate. Their voices echoed to the bottom and back up along the walls/crags.

They navigated several hundred metres, winding through narrow passages, some letting through only slivers of light to guide them forwards. They filed left and right, avoiding the jagged edges and small fragments of rock that were tumbling from the sides here and there. At that moment their view opened out to see the coastline once again in the distance and a gust of wind brought fresh air into their reach.

As they emerged, they loosened their scarves and took in the view. The sky was a vibrant blue, softened only by the occasional wayward cloud. The wind appeared to have chased any others away and so our party needed to manoeuvre carefully to land at a nearby beach.

Once safely on the ground, they fixed their packs, rehydrated and poised once again to take in their surroundings. They were once again struck by the stark absence of life. There was a soft silence within the small, secluded ocean cove pierced only by the sound of the waves crashing on the shoreline. Ellianon suggested they rest for a while and laid out a large blanket on which he also placed several supplies of tea and cookies. Everyone shared the rations gratefully, munching away at the chocolate chips whilst gazing around at the beautiful spot in which they'd found themselves. This gave them the appetite to investigate a little.

Inalia removed her boots, rolled up the bottoms of her trousers and waded a short way into the sea. She stood there looking out towards the horizon as the waves crashed over her ankles. Not a sign of life in sight. The expanse of dark blue moving in curls of deep swell. She could hear the sound of each wave crashing on the beach behind her. The repetition would continue and continue, probably forever, whether she was there or not and she suddenly felt the strength of New Earth's resilience. She had only been living for an instant compared to the age of the Earth. The waves had been caressing these shores for as long as time could remember and they would continue to do so even after she was long gone. She felt the same sense of inner calm that she had also felt when Castedon had shown them the exercise to be in their heart spaces. She was filled with the simplicity of the moment, feeling the waves lap around her.

The silence was broken by Bethanor calling from behind them. He'd found an area at the base of the cliff side that was also starting to regenerate. Everyone hurried excitedly to see. There were pools of seawater that were being replenished regularly by the high tide, within which small sea creatures could be seen moving around and going about their business. What was interesting was the fact that there was a small ecosystem forming around this life as they were depositing remnants of food and shells on the beach and clearly they spent time digging in the sand. There was seaweed and small plants growing up the side of the rocks. A few metres up in the cliff side there was even a bird's nest carefully harboured into a space between two rocks. Our friends looked excitedly at one another. This was the sign of hope they had been waiting for. There was life here despite what everyone had told them back home in Reviathan.

Castedon and Kalto carefully analysed a few samples, placing them delicately in special air-tight boxes ready to be examined when they returned to their respective laboratories.

They then all formed a seated circle within this area and sent positive intentions to the surrounding space. They picked up certain elements of the rocklike substances on which the vegetation was growing and recomposed more of them them to support the regeneration that was already underway, taking care not to touch the plants themselves. Sparks are not of course allowed to impact anything living with their powers. Each living organism had the free will to live according to its own plan and it is forbidden to tamper with the energy fields or physical matter of any other living thing. In spite of their differences, Sparks all agreed to this basic respect of living things. The vegetation would take the time of the natural cycles of life to grow and proliferate again.

The sun was starting to lower towards the West so with a firm nod, Ellianon indicated to the group that it was time to return back to Reviathan or they would not be back there in time for sunset. They imagined how amazing it would be to experience a sunset in this secluded area but they knew that their parents would be waiting for them and more importantly that they would ask many questions if they returned too late. As they looked around one last time, they all hoped that there would be another opportunity in future to continue exploring New Earth. They felt so moved by seeing the emergence of life that it was difficult to pull themselves away. Castedon beckoned encouragingly.

Back-packs were filled, bodies hydrated and the Regsters were charged up with enough power for the return trip. In no time, the group had parted ways, wishing Ellianon well with his search for the Tree of Justice that they had seen in the Enadon's vision. He would be heading past the Northern mountain range where there was still a small sprinkling of snow on the peaks, despite the harsh arid environment at their base. He had enough supplies for three days although it should only take him another full day depending on where he camped for the night. He had spent a lot of time with the group and now he would need to make up for that in order to move across the plains to an area that could provide him with sufficient shelter.

A line was quickly formed as the group filed back one

after the other through the ravine. There were now more shadows forming down the cliff sides. With less light, everyone needed to be extra careful to avoid the jutting rock faces. As they rounded a bend they were startled to see the Enadon swoop right past them and upwards to circle above their heads. An instant later it had disappeared over the top edge of the ravine.

Castedon indicated to everyone to increase the throttle and swing round ninety degrees to follow it. Surprisingly it had perched on the far edge of a group of nearby rocks, waiting for them to approach. As they did so, it swung around, unfurling its enormous, scaled wings and swooped up towards the air once again, flying off towards the Northern mountains. Perhaps Ellianon would see it too. Perhaps it would guide him to the place they had seen in their vision?

Just as they were contemplating the significance of this second encounter, Inalia looked down at where the Enadon had been perched, only to see a small pile of rubble. Everyone fired down their Regsters to stop for a moment. Normally, rubble wouldn't be interesting but the final, dying flames of a fire were dancing in between the charcoaled sticks of wood. Someone else had been here and judging by the scene they had left behind, their presence was very recent, perhaps even within the past hour. The fire glowed and in its reflection, the group could see food left overs, a fish along with footprints both circling and extending from the fire towards what looked like a path leading behind the rocks. Castedon was extremely curious but at the same time, encouraged everyone to be cautious. Sparks were rarely found bare-footed, although this was New Earth after all so was there such a thing as usual? Castedon was the first to follow the trail, carefully, footprint after footprint. They were human footprints, no doubt about that. Were there more than one person? It was difficult to say.

They followed one after the other beyond the rocks cautiously. It was so silent you could almost hear everyone's hearts racing. As the dusk light touched the other side, they stumbled on a small array of rocks positioned in a platform-like structure, and with it, more half-eaten fish remains. They approached the scene hesitantly, when something struck them, the view from there was directly overlooking the valley where they had been only minutes earlier. Whoever was here could have been watching them! Inalia felt a shiver run down her spine. Everyone looked at one another, then left and right, but there was no-one else in sight.

"Time to leave," said Castedon abruptly reminding himself that he wasn't alone and had committed to bringing the group back to the safety of Reviathan. He turned and led everyone back towards their intended trajectory, indicating to them to quietly fire up their Regsters and be on their way. Bethanor couldn't help but look behind him as they filed off into the distance, one after the other. The ground was silent.

As they landed once again at Reviathan's borders, everyone took a moment to regain their composure, folding their Regsters. Dusk had ceded to a starry night sky and fire flies were weaving their way between the trees.

"What was that all about?" Asked Kalto.

"I'm not quite sure what to make of it," replied Castedon as they set off walking back to Sector Four. "I have heard rumours of others having seen footprints but there is no real idea as to who these people are. It's very strange to see them with our own eyes."

"Ouf!" the group heard Kalto give a muffled echo in the background.

"You see according to our calculations," Castedon continued "It would be next to impossible for anyone to have survived the cataclysm without evacuating to Reviathan."

Castedon turned towards his friends. "Kalto? Where's Kalto?" enquired Castedon a little puzzled.
"Down here!" They heard a resounding call from a nearby ditch where Kalto was hauling himself out again looking rather embarrassed, a large group of curious fire flies circling around him.

"I just wanted a closer look at them" he said sheepishly.

The group giggled, helping Kalto back to his feet again.

"Ok, it's been a long day. Definitely time to head home for you all! We can speak tomorrow," added Castedon.

Chapter Six

The Experiment

On their arrival to the Western district, Kalto and Inalia touch together all five fingertips as is the custom and leave Bethanor to his thoughts close to the hideout. He knew he should return home but the pull was just too strong to go there for a while and investigate the new materials which he had carefully stored there. Despite being tired from the day's adventures, time was also ticking before he had to complete his project for the rite of passage. He had decomposed each of them and wanted to see if they could be combined with other ingredients that he already had to hand there. Even though his intuition was telling him to return home, his curiosity got the better of him. The old door swung open and Bethanor lunged himself into the comfiest chair and sank down. It had been a very long and emotionally tiring day. Here he could resource, hiding from the world just for a moment. Bethanor never spent long stretches of time alone. It wasn't something that he enjoyed. Contact with others, like for most Sparks was fundamental, but every once in a while he needed to take a step back to feel what was right when a situation was confusing him. He slowly went over the events of the day in his mind, recalling all that had been said, the excitement, the questions, the devastation of New Earth. He felt quite saturated and to be honest a little shaken by the discovery of the camp.

What was it? Could it mean there were actually people on New Earth? Were they Seasons or nomadic Stars. If so, why would they have been watching them? He looked at the pictures he had taken of the footprints.

Then he thought about how grateful he was that Ellianon and Castedon had taken them there. How open and generous they had been. He was almost taken aback by how welcome he'd felt in the Eastern Suburbs these past two days. He'd always been told that it was an obscure place and that recluses were potentially dangerous whereas he'd felt quite the opposite. Why would we segregate like that only based on slightly different viewpoints of how to create? I guess it was so fundamental to their identity but was it important enough to create division within the Sparks Tribe? These Sparks were actually very courageous, dedicating their lives to their beliefs which seemed pretty altruistic. Bethanor could not fathom what had brought his tribe to distance like that when one of their most important values was togetherness. He could not see how the Sparks were all living according to their values. "What irony" he thought "we value togetherness and yet we are divided. We value creativity and yet we try to control". He resolved to discuss the question with his mother, hoping of course that she would not sense that they had taken a detour into the Eastern Suburbs, never mind New Earth.

As he sat there in the stillness, he turned the Chromavelia around, contemplating its shape and colour. It had a particularly strange base mix of a green and copper hues but with each colour refracting through a clear quartz layer. He decomposed and recomposed it gently, twisting and turning it into different shapes.

"What should I combine it with?" Bethanor mused. He would need to remove any unvalidated or potentially unstable molecules, hopefully still keeping the greenish-copper hue. "That would give a very unique finish to my sculpture," he concluded "Ok let's think."

"How about combining with lithium? or Orium? What would that do?" His mind raced. "What about if I combined it with F563?". "The property that makes it unstable is most likely the rapid conduction of the Helianteel molecules but I don't need the conduction properties anyway. Let's get rid of those first," he thought "Then I can test different combinations without much difficulty."

First he would test the quality and level of vibration of the light that came out of the mineral to monitor exactly what happened. The sun wasn't too strong at this time of day and there were no rain showers due. Conditions were in fact pretty good. He separated off a small piece of the Chromavelia.

Looking around, he noticed a rather flat rock which would serve well as a solid base to support the experiment. He turned the Chromavelia in several directions before placing it on a side which had just two flat segments, the others having more hexagonal projections emanating from them. The reflections were so beautiful on the surrounding greenery, even reflecting up the side of a nearby Eucalyptus tree which now looked to be glowing a luminous apple green. Bethanor watched intently and his excitement grew as the indicator on his gauge swung beyond the 80 gamma level of light quality, the sound fuser that he had placed next to it was pulsing the light rays 3 or 4 metres into the environment around it. His focus was so intent on measuring the vibrational level that he did not notice that the innermost core of the mineral fragment had begun to smoke. And it continued. As it grew in intensity, so did the internal pressure. The light continued to refract through until suddenly there was an almighty crack and an explosion of green light resounded across the main square. It startled many passers by and two men ran towards Bethanor to help contain any danger.

Bethanor was shocked but managed to dive for cover. As the men arrived he rolled over into a half crouch and wiped his hands over his face in disbelief. Despite all of his calculations, he hadn't expected a reaction of the sort. One of the men covered the remaining Chomavelia with his cape and joined the other man to check on Bethanor who had raised himself to his knees.

Bethanor, who was already rather a proud character was feeling a distinct feeling of embarrassment. He'd only wanted to verify a small step of his experiment before returning home and now the entire square was focused on his mishap.

"Are you ok?" asked the man closest to him.

"Yes, I guess," replied Bethanor "just surprised."

"All well?" asked the second man. "What was that?" he asked inquisitively.

"Just something I found that I was testing," said Bethanor even more sheepishly.

"Hmmm, let me guess, it was an off-list element?" the man continued. "You realise how dangerous that is? That is why the committee spends so much time validating the Molecular Register. I won't report the incident but I think your parents should be aware so you can discuss this together" the man continued "Who are your parents?"

"Zenalis and Aperion, right?" added the other man who was tending to Bethanor.

"Right" replied Bethanor quietly.

"I know them well" the second man replied, "I will accompany you home."
The first man nodded and turned to leave. He presented his five fingertips to Bethanor and the second man to

show his respect as he departed. Bethanor touched his as a mark of his own respect and thanked the man for coming to his aid. Meanwhile the second man was recovering his cape and the offending object from the nearby rock. It was still warm and smoking slightly but given that the light could no longer penetrate, it was safe to transport.

"Shall we go?" offered the man, nodding towards the direction of Bethanor's house.

Bethanor rose to his feet, brushed himself down and set off by the side of the helpful stranger.

"How do you know my parents?" he asked as they crossed the edge of the main square.

"Old school friends," he replied. "Let's just say it's been for many years. Lorin, pleased to meet you. And you must be Bethanor?"

Being escorted back home made Bethanor feel very small, even if Lorin was well-intentioned and he knew that it was only to be expected. It felt like a very big contrast to the freedom he had felt that morning in the Eastern Suburbs. He'd felt that his questions and opinions had been taken seriously and that he'd be free to explore. As soon as he was back home in the Western Suburbs, it was very different and despite the fact that he understood the impact of his actions in testing the Chromavelia, for a moment he felt like an incompetent.

His mother opened the door in her usual warm, welcoming way, smiling widely at Lorin and especially at seeing that he was accompanied by Bethanor.

"Hello my dear" she said embracing Bethanor gently.

Bethanor smiled back but she could not help but notice the unease in his posture.

"Hello Zenalis," said Lorin, "It is lovely to see you again after so long. How is your research?"

"Still thoroughly enjoying my investigations thank you and I believe we are making progress in rebuilding some of the marine life diversity that we lost as a result of the early stages of the ecological cataclysm. The coral replanting and regeneration in collaboration with the Seasons Tribe is proving most effective. We are continuing to benefit from all of the work that had been started before the disaster and we have been able to apply the same early techniques. It was so fortunate for us that there were such forward-thinking people, prepared to invest in regenerating the reefs. We have learnt a lot from them". Her enthusiasm was indeed still evident as her eyes sparkled with excitement in sharing her positive news. "And how are you Lorin? I am delighted to see you. What brings you to our home?"

Lorin paused for a moment. "I am very well thank you,

and the Youngers are growing well. We recently started a family project to extend the permaculture boxes in the kitchen. Everyone is participating and it is flourishing so I am feeling very blessed". The man took a small breath and then continued "Zenalis, I have accompanied Bethanor because we have some information to share with you concerning an event in the main square earlier this evening. Bethanor, do you wish to share?". Bethanor couldn't help but roll his eyes, looking for somewhere to place his line of vision without having to look directly at his mother.

"I was testing a new element that I came upon when I visited the Eastern Suburbs this morning. It caused a minor explosion which Lorin helped to contain." Bethanor continued "As is customary, Lorin accompanied me to ensure it was known to you."

Lorin smiled benevolently. Zenalis took in a short breath as if to compose herself following the surprise announcement.

"Ok," she said gently but firmly. "What is this material and why were you in the Eastern Suburbs this morning?"

"I believe it is called Chromavelia," said Bethanor "It's a mix of Helianteel and Stroic which is embedded in clear quartz".

Zenalis nodded knowingly and encouragingly for her son

to continue.

"I went to the Eastern Suburbs because I was curious and started to think about the tear in the Aurora layer and how it could be repaired." Bethanor took a moment and then continued "I guess my curiosity and enthusiasm got the better of me."

"Well I will leave you to continue discussing," said Lorin. "I am very pleased to have met you Bethanor. Be attentive with your experiments."

He raised his hand to touch fingertips with both Bethanor and Zenalis and turned to continue going about his business. There was an awkward silence.

"Let's go inside and sit down shall we?" said Zenalis.

Bethanor followed her cautiously, wondering how this was all going to turn out. It had to be said that he rarely was caught doing anything that he shouldn't, and he was almost proud of his track record. He didn't feel so proud today though, even if it felt like an injustice to part of him.

They both sat down on the cushioned bench under the permaculture box. Zenalis was quiet and she looked inquisitively at Bethanor.

"What were you looking for that you couldn't find

here?" she asked.

"I just felt a need to explore," replied Bethanor "I was looking at the Alpha Light Network and it seemed that most of the conventional avenues had been investigated. I wanted to find something new."

"I understand," empathised Zenalis "You wanted to explore further and your curiosity led you in new directions?"

"Yes," replied Bethanor "I feel so restricted sometimes, decomposing and recomposing the same things. I'm seventeen and I feel like I've been doing that forever! It seems like everyone still thinks I'm five years old sometimes and can't be trusted. I have so little space to create that I feel suffocated. Like my creativity is so boxed."

"In what way?" Zenalis questioned.

"Why do we restrict so many materials that could really help us to solve some important problems? The cataclysm created an extraordinary amount of damage and the tear in the Aurora Belt is widening. It feels like we're turning a blind eye to so much potential? We're Sparks, we create, that's what we do! Why don't we let ourselves create freely rather than from a checklist of items that everyone has used before?" Bethanor was becoming quite animated.

"I see, so this is why you went to the Eastern Suburbs? Specifically to find materials off the official committee list?" questioned Zenalis.

"I just wanted to look around," said Bethanor "I wasn't actually planning to buy anything, it just happened. I'd never seen anything like the Chromavelia before and I just know that the refraction could create an amazing effect for a sculpture. Don't you think it's feasible?"

"It isn't my place to suppose anything of the materials outside of the official list Bethanor, this list is validated for a reason. All the materials on it are subjected to rigorous testing to avoid the type of problem that you had earlier this evening. Can you imagine if everyone created their own rules and tested any of the materials that we receive from other dimensions from the Star Tribes or the relics that the Seasons Tribe find? We have no idea what they could do."

"But if we create from our heart spaces? In the Eastern Suburbs they speak of an unwritten code to which everyone adheres and that is they never create anything which lowers themselves or humanity as a whole so none of their creations are ever carried out for selfish reasons of glory or money. Did you know that many of the so called recluses are Sparks who have worked for many years at the research labs. They apply the same rigorous testing procedures."

"Yes I know," replied Zenalis quietly. "And what of those who do not? The recluses, the rebels who just wish to create without any limits? It is for this reason that they choose to be out of the city limits also."

"I think they understand that their work is more volatile, they just don't want to be treated like second class citizens, like they are rejected by society because of their different beliefs."

Zenalis paused. "We do not consider them second class," she maintained "Most left in objection to the listings and refused to return. The committee simply said that those who lived within the confines of the city would also be responsible to their community by applying their creativity through the Molecular Register and not wider. It has served us well for the past 25 years. Whilst ever the recluses behave in an unresponsible way, they will not be allowed to practice within the city boundaries." She seemed somewhat saddened.

"Why do we segregate?" continued Bethanor "Our values are of togetherness, Sparks need contact, connection with others. I do not understand. We live so divided?"

"It is to protect the little that remains of our people Bethanor. I wish it could be another way. A very small minority endanger our very existence with their practices. At present there is no solution. For now I do not wish that you venture back into the Eastern Suburbs for this reason and I hope you will respect the rules that we live by. You are almost of age and your choices reflect in your behaviour by respecting yourself and those around you. Please choose wisely my beloved son. As for the Chromavelia, I will place it in safe-keeping at the laboratory. They will do with it as they see fit."

Bethanor fell silent. His mother kissed his forehead and left the room without another word. He was left with his thoughts spinning, wondering what to do next. He wanted to tell her about the footprints but he wasn't even supposed to be in the Eastern Suburbs, let alone New Earth. In any case she wouldn't believe him. Perhaps no-one would, there are no people in New Earth after all. "But I know what I saw" Bethanor reassured himself. Should he abandon all his dreams or could he find another way that still respects his mother's wishes? He pondered the question for a moment and then went to his room to rest. It had been a long day.

Chapter Seven

The Return of the Recluse

Bethanor woke with a start, the light was streaming through the blinds in his room and it must have been at least 10 a.m. He had slept deeply but what startled him was not the light but an idea that had just appeared vividly in his mind. He had seen an image of a network of many connected colours running between the pockets of discussion in the Eastern Suburbs. The image had been clear in his mind and he was left with a deep sense of purpose, of knowing the right thing to do. Perhaps he could stay in contact with some of the researchers of the Eastern Suburbs without actually going there? His mother hadn't asked him to abandon his research after all. The Alpha Light Network was officially open to everyone... perhaps they could all contribute to a new direction of investigation? How could they be a part of all those fruitful daily discussions and the intensive research that was going on over there in order that they could all work together to solve the Aurora Belt problem? Perhaps he could initiate another direction of research on the network and interview different people he had met in order to share their work with the rest of the network? That way they could continue their search virtually from the hideout, connecting that part of the Tribe back into the main hub and perhaps other people would then test the new materials instead of Bethanor!

He sprung to his feet, pulled on a sweater, pants and boots and was out of the door in a matter of minutes. No time to clean up! Discussing this idea with Inalia and Kalto was more important! From his Messagepad he called for his friends to meet him there but he didn't wait for their arrival to set about investigating how he could put his idea into action.

He opened the network connection and looked for a branch of the data that he could open out. One that would make sense to other people to hook onto. Should he mention the Chromavelia? Or the Violet Enigma? He scanned the matrix of data, left and right, every branch for the best way in to expand their search. There were at least three sections that could be good possibilities. Where would it lead the research if he opened branches there? Bethanor paced the floor as he thought about it.

In his mind, the problem only hadn't already been resolved because either it would require investigating materials that had not yet been explored, and that wasn't an option, or everyone was looking in the wrong place.

"Perhaps rather than concentrating on repairing the tear directly as most of the research teams were, we should concentrate our efforts on reversing the origin of the problems?" thought Bethanor. "Let's investigate the causes instead of the effects."

He had heard that the toxic gases were created by plants. They could alternatively talk first about the toxic plants and work backwards from there perhaps. He decided that it would be best to break with the existing body of research in order to open a new question asking *"Why did these plants affect the atmosphere in such a detrimental way? What was different about them?"*

As Inalia came through he door she could sense the excitement in the room and see the anticipation in Bethanor's face.

"Inalia. What if we extend the Alpha Light Network with a new branch of research?" he asked. "What if we invite the researchers to contribute their amazing work to our think tank?"

He was almost not breathing between sentences.

"What if we organised virtual sessions to connect people together to have the same discussions as in the Eastern Suburbs, every Friday morning, we could share in the ideas and investigations that they have carried out during the week without even having to go there. We have contacts now, we can do this!" he enthused.

"Yes," cried Inalia "We can also shine a light on the work that they're doing. Show everyone that they are careful and altruistic and not at all as reckless as we're told! Do you think they'd help?" she added.

"We won't know until we ask them," replied Bethanor.

She lowered the Co-Lab screen so they could start to draw up some plans and just at that moment Kalto arrived looking still half asleep.

"Hey guys! What's flowing?" he asked curiously seeing through the morning blur that his friends were actually deeply immersed in a creative thinking session.

"We're planning to create a new branch of research on why the plants are so toxic and we're going to ask everyone in the Eastern Suburbs to contribute," launched Bethanor.

"Do you think they'll let you?" replied Kalto dubiously.

"Only one way to find out!" added Inalia with a big smile.

The network was vast and the combinations were already numerous. As they scanned through, they noticed that in 2066 someone had started to investigate the plants.

"Composition, light capture and photosynthesis," Bethanor read the sections out loud "This looks perfect!"

"Secondary effects of the toxicity of the plants...." he continued and then stopped dead in his tracks. The section was tagged with a name, one that he recognized… He pointed to his friends who acknowledged with surprise. *Castedon.*

The Co-Lab screen blinked light blue flashes as it connected to Castedon's local Messagepad captor. His face appeared in the middle of the screen, smiling as always.

"Good morning my friends," he started "How are you all?"

For a moment they all stared, not quite knowing what to say. How was his name in the network? It was Inalia who broke the silence, the suspense was killing her.

"Castedon, we'd like your help," she opened. "We decided to open a branch in the Network to continue investigating the tear in the atmospheric layer. Our dream is to include all the discussions that are happening on this subject in the Eastern Suburbs and expose the great work that Argolia and others are doing."

Castedon's eyes sparked with intrigue. "Go on," he encouraged.

"We can formulate everything that is written into a co-created, synthesized version of the different layers and colours of discussion. Since we're not from the Eastern Suburbs people might believe us when we find an interesting angle of investigation," said Bethanor enthusiastically. "Each week we want to share any revelations from the discussions that happen between all of us. Will you help us?"

Castedon looked away from the screen for a moment. "What makes you think that they will listen?" he asked, sounding a little sceptical, as his face also became more serious.

"I guess we don't know for sure but we can only try," said Kalto "No-one sees their work today. The answer might be right under our noses!"

"True enough," replied Castedon, he paused for a moment looking at their enthusiasm. "What would you like me to do?" he replied supportively.

"To start with, will you share with us why your name is tagged in the network with the research on the toxic plants? That's exactly where we wanted to hook in," asked Bethanor rather directly.

There was another short silence as Castedon went into his thoughts.

"I see," he said after a moment and a knowing smile returned. "So you want to analyse the moment when everything changed? When the plants switched from being inoffensive? I also wanted to understand why such a drastic change and in particular why no-one was even looking there. I was asked to stop."

"By who?" asked Inalia indignantly.

"Let's just say that within the group that were investigating, we didn't all agree on what to search for. I wanted to explore all the options available to us and another man blocked us. He was a Committee member so it was easy for him. He insisted that we stay within the limits of researching more deeply what the mainstream scientists were saying at the time. Plus he wanted us to only use the list of validated materials from the Molecular Register, which had just been created a few years earlier so was pretty small at the time. It didn't give us much to work with and my view was that we were overly restricting ourselves. Just because no-one has yet discovered or *validated* something's existence it does not mean that it does not *actually* exist and nature does not have a place for it. We just don't know how to describe so many materials because they are not within our frame of current understanding. Our decomposition abilities do have some limits, but I never really believed in restricting the possibilities for finding a solution to something as important as this. So after a very noisy, visible debate we agreed to disagree and I left for the Eastern Suburbs where I could live and study in harmony with like-minded people. I left my research open exactly where it finished on the Network. Sometimes people just have a different way of looking at life, at what is acceptable or not. It's a difficult balance to find, and our people are still searching for a good solution."

Our friends looked back at Castedon with warm, supportive empathy. The question was, would they find themselves in the same situation?

"Perhaps the situation has evolved by now," reassured Castedon seeing the concern in their eyes. "It was twenty years ago don't forget," he paused. "I will support you" he concluded "Tell me what you need from me."

The discussion between them evolved left and right, with ideas, crescendos, false hopes and new ideas emerging. The group discussed directions of investigation, who to involve, how to encourage them to share, and how to communicate regularly? Inalia was to coordinate the recovery of the week's information for the network, Castedon to evangelise the idea with the key researchers of the Eastern Suburbs. Others would then be welcomed to contribute ideas and resources. Kalto would be responsible for consolidating their findings into the network, tagging and structuring the information collected and Bethanor would prepare the discussion with the Committee and oversee the overall coherence and progress of the research with Castedon's help.

Excitement reigned. Bethanor was convinced by the opportunity of brining some new perspectives on the issue. Part of him was also inspired and relieved to know that Castedon had thought of looking in the same direction all those years ago. Surely there must be something there? He felt they could make something big happen this time.

On the first Friday morning of the meetings as our friends arrived at the hideout they felt a sense of nervous anticipation. They lowered the co-lab screen and scanned the agenda for their meeting with the Eastern Suburbs. As the visual blinked open, they saw Castedon with the jade lady. They appeared calm and receptive. Behind them, to their surprise was a room full of Sparks sitting in small groups discussing. They all seemed to be in a large open space where these groups were gathered together exchanging in an animated fashion. Notes were being taken, people were displaying and analysing different materials which were being decomposed and merged in front of their eyes. Energy shifting and recreating new form in the spirit of togetherness and a quest for understanding and improving. Bethanor felt both proud and moved by the scene. These were his tribe giving freely to support the project.

"We've been here since 6 a.m.," introduced Castedon, "When we spoke about the project to different people they were motivated to join us, to add the research they have carried out and support finding a solution. Everyone agrees that this problem has been menacing humanity for far too long. There are over 40 researchers here whom I know personally. They will help us openly and they know that we can do more together."

The friends were amazed at the big turn out. They had hoped for help but this was astounding. Inalia wondered how she was going to recover all of their contributions without missing any vital element. "Perhaps this was bigger than they could manage?" she thought. She took three deep breaths as she noticed her anxious feelings and sure enough she started to feel more reassured and her confidence returned "No we can manage this. We have all the support we need."

As the meeting started, they recapped the project's intention "*to investigate the source of the plants' toxicity*". In no time they were in deep conversation with each of the volunteers. Some had studied the plants' reactivity for some time and their interaction with their surroundings. They were submerging the banks of the rivers of New Earth, and the waste they were expulsing was not allowing any oxygen to pass through the surface of certain stagnant areas of water. When this happened, the soil around the banks became putrid and all life-forms in the vicinity had been badly impacted. The water here was evaporating during warm days causing toxic rayadon gases to rise into the atmosphere. It was carried high and far by the violence of the sandstorms. The plants themselves were beautiful which is why they had raised little concern up till now. White flowers sprouting along winding vines of many metres. With the rise in temperature after the cataclysm, they were reproducing at a rapid rate.

Some of the researchers had been documenting the lands for some time and sent over detailed pictures of their anatomy along with precise maps of how their coverage has spread in certain areas of New Earth. One researcher was even measuring the relationship between the quantity of plants, the amount of rayadon gases in the environment around them and the size of the tear in the atmosphere around the Aurora Belt. He was delighted to be able to share his findings as no-one was taking his analysis seriously. One after the other, the researchers patiently and clearly explained their hypotheses, the approaches used for their research and their findings. They showed many materials that they were using to investigate the interaction of the plants with their environment. What could recover balance within this ecosystem?

Inalia was busily integrating all the data and regenerating notes using the co-lab thought enabler functionality. It was starting to look like quite a comprehensive study of the plants themselves and their habitat. Some elements seemed like they didn't quite interlink she noticed as the co-lab tool traced relationships between the different elements.

"Still parts to investigate," she indicated to Bethanor, pointing to gaps in the data. "What is the critical temperature causing the plants to become dangerous? The reason the plants are there in the first place? We need wider visibility of their locations... but it's looking pretty good," she said encouragingly.

Kalto was busily transcribing the in-depth research results into the network... "rayadon gases.... plants impacted by rises in temp... oops!" he said loudly looking up as the Co-Lab screen blipped and shut down for an instant in front of Inalia's eyes.

"What? *No!*" she exclaimed, then looking over at Kalto "That wasn't funny," she said as Kalto flipped the screen back on laughing heartily to himself. Inalia continued to summerize all of the elements as the conversations continued.

As they shared the amazing joint progress in the research, the group set their intention to continue to review more of the elements over the coming week. The researchers were both amazed and motivated by the common threads in their work. For many it was their life passion to solve this issue and they were inspired by the possibility to work together. The co-creation session was convened until the following Friday, with Bethanor and Castedon thanking the participants in the usual manner. It was a job well done and still another 10 days before the Committee meeting!

That afternoon Kalto suggested that they go out into the mountains. It was a beautiful day and the crystal clear blue sky opened out above them. Just a few clouds filled the haze like whips of cotton candy. They fixed their intention on the horizon and started out. A few hundred meters into the walk Bethanor stopped and looked at his friends.

"Why don't we go back to New Earth, look around a bit more? We learnt so much last time. I'm sure it will help our research. What do you think?" he said without really thinking about it.

Inalia and Kalto looked at each other for a moment, their hearts started racing. "Don't we need to go with Castedon or Ellianon?" asked Inalia.

"Ellianon won't be back for another day at least," said Bethanor "We don't have so much time before the Committee meeting."

"What if we get lost? You know we're not supposed to go there," said Inalia.

"We can say we took a wrong turn," said Kalto laughing loudly.

"Over the frontier? *Really*?" said Inalia looking sarcastically at Kalto who hunched his shoulders.

"We don't need to go far and we can take extra food provisions and a security flare in case we need to call for attention if it makes you feel more comfortable Inalia? I think it's a great idea. My parents are away until tomorrow so we could say we're staying at my place!"

"That would give us time to do some research when we get back too, excellent!" said Bethanor "Let's do it!"

"Ok," shrugged Inalia.

They veered left in the road in order to head back to the hideout. They needed to gather more provisions and protective clothing but they were soon on their way again. Their excited anticipation grew with each step.

"Which way should we go this time? Same direction?" questioned Bethanor.

"Why don't we head South? Not far, just enough to see if it's any different? We can track our way using the radars on our Messagepads," suggested Kalto.

"*If they work!*" said Inalia again sarcastically.

"Well we"ll just stop and turn around if they don't," said Kalto shaking his head as he sensed that Inalia was trying to find excuses, "And you can always stay here if you like…," he added making fun of her.
"Ok so we go South," said Bethanor

The party set out on their Regsters once again, Kalto being especially careful this time to take enough time to find his balance. They stayed close and as they approached the frontier they remained in the shadows. It would be difficult to recognize them with their scarves wrapped around their heads to prevent the sand from entering, only their eyes could be discerned, but they were nervous all the same. Bethanor could feel his stomach twisting and turning. This was serious, choosing to go themselves was their responsibility, there was no possibility of saying they were invited by Elianon or Castedon. Inalia admitted that she felt a bit sick with anxiety.

The way towards New Earth stretched out far into the horizon, with resting platforms every hundreds metres or so in case of any difficulties. It was really to show the direction to New Earth since everyone had Regsters these days anyway. And there were problems. Sometimes the Regsters would cut out in mid-ocean, at which point their safety throttle would hopefully kick-in but there were accidents and people were known to have drowned crossing over the threshold according to the stories of the Eastern Suburbs.

Kalto led the way, using his sense of humour to keep the atmosphere as light as possible. "Do you think we should bring back fish for dinner? Cod or tuna? Wait…there's a huge one looking right at me from down there! I can see its big bulging eyes looking right at me!"

At each platform he let his Regster run underneath while he jumped over, each time performing a different trick -

somersaults, star jumps…. Inalia laughed, which made her forget her nervousness. Bethanor was busy thinking about the adventure ahead, imagining the path they'd take.

The sun was hidden behind a hazy mist of sand storm which became more dense as they approached the shoreline. Kalto pulled his scarf tighter, even closer to his eyes to prevent the sand entering. He squinted, trying to make out the way ahead.

They lined the coast to the South. The rugged cliff faces jutted out over the rough sea causing spray to rise up high into the air engulfing a mass of the sand storm with each new wave. Our group would need to be careful to avoid slipping and besides, any wet clothes would mean that the sand would stick, forming a heavy paste that would weigh them down.

Around two kilometres further along the coast, Kalto halted close to the shelter of two old broken trees. He could hear a faint humming which sounded like it might be coming from the motor of his Regster. He unhooked his supplies and knelt down on the barren, desolate ground next to the faltering contraption feeling somewhat bewildered. As he inspected the ventilation outlet, his gaze was hijacked as he noticed what looked like footprints in the earth. One, two, many of them. They appeared to lead towards a nearby cavern entrance and like last time there was no sign of shoes. He called over

Inalia and Bethanor to inspect them more closely. Could they be Sparks? They paused looking for a decent landmark in order to find their bearings. The sun was still positioned to the East so it must have been around 10am.

"What do you think?" Asked Kalto

"Castedon said that Sparks don't travel barefoot," said Inalia starting to shift from one foot to the other "This is too weird. I think we should turn back."

Bethanor looked at her and smiled ironically. "Seriously?" he said "This is great! I thought we came looking for adventure? Well here it is and you want to go home?"

Inalia looked a little sheepish then replied "Well it is weird isn't it? Did you ever meet anyone who doesn't wear shoes?"

"Should we follow them?" said Kalto "They lead towards the cavern over there."

The party folded away their Regsters and slowly approached the entrance of the cave. As the mid-morning light penetrated inside they could see rows and rows of stalactites and stalagmites protruding from the ceiling and floor in front of them. Their form was both eerie and beautiful. They projected shadows across the ancient walls and across the path ahead that they started to follow cautiously. There was something distinctly heavy about the atmosphere inside and a musty smell was lingering around them that made it hard to breathe.

With a swipe of the hand, Inalia captured a sample of the air in her left hand and lifted it to analyse the contents. The elements swirled around breaking into twists of blues, yellows and browns as she decomposed them.

"Contains oxygen, a micro amounts of nitrogen, hydrogen sulphide and several traces of sulphur," she said to the others, squinting into the swirling mix. "Best not to light any fires in here would be my advice," she said with a half-smile.

She released the gasses back into the atmosphere with another wave of the hand, at the same time transforming it back into its original form.

The party moved forward with a sense of caution. The footprints were becoming less clear and the light dimmed away from the entrance, but after all there was only one path to follow. They could hear dripping in the distance, slow but constant and as they turned a slippery corner, they started to hear the quiet sound of water brushing up against some rocks. There was light at the far side of what looked like a small estuary in front of them, leading back out to the sea. The ceiling of the cave loomed several metres above their heads which made them all at once feel rather small. The sound of their feet moving along the path suddenly started to echo around them. They stopped in their tracks and looked around trying to calm their anxiety and yet satisfy their curiosity.

Behind some rocks to the right they could make out the back of what seemed like it might be some kind of boat, two of them. They were floating at least, and were attached together bobbing gently as the tide swung in and out. They clearly belonged to someone. Bethanor felt a chill run down his spine. Their gazes were busy analysing every millimetre of the cave and their minds raced with stories of who and what might be there.

"There are people living here," whispered Kalto "I just knew it! They said there was no one living on New Earth! They lied to us. I don't know what kind of boat it is but it's certainly not designed by a Spark that's for sure."

"Shhhh," said Inalia "They might hear us."

The cave once again became filled with an eerie silence. Only impacted by the ebbing and flowing of the waves. Our friends were still anxious, acting like deer having heard the sound of a nearby lion, and not knowing what to do next. Their eyes wide, they looked at each other for cues. "The boats" beckoned Bethanor as he moved to board one carefully to take a look round. Inalia and Kalto followed closely behind watching their step. They were indeed very strange, almond-shaped made of what re-sembled wood and metal panels and plating.

"Doesn't look very aerodynamic or hydrodynamic," said Kalto "Where are the composites? Amazed they get it to float!" he said in a mocking voice.

"What if we gave it a go?" suggested Bethanor "See how it works."

His curiosity was beginning to take over as he strided around on the waiting vessel.

"Can't go very fast," reassured Inalia "and I guess if there was anyone here they would have come out by now. Ok let's go!"

"The boat? Yeah, sure, might function better than my Regster," Kalto laughed "Even if it does look like an old dumpster."

The interior was sparse. There were supplies lying strewn around that could only be described as primitive, definitely pre-cataclysm: a fishing rod, an old mobile phone, and two metal containers that probably used to carry food supplies. Kalto had seen them in the labs brought in by the Seasons who had found them.

"They can't work anymore, there are no networks, the Snow Tribe have upgraded all the connections across the

communication network," said Inalia "Why would anyone keep one of these archaic things?" She questioned as
she turned it over and over in her hand. "This just gets
stranger."

"It looks like if we pull here…..vroom… there is a motor
in there." Bethanor fell backwards, slightly startled, that
it actually worked.

"Yes that's a motor alright," said Kalto trying to contain
his laughter in case it offended Bethanor. "What is it using for energy?" He asked.

"Some kind of ancient fluid fuel by the smell of it," said
Inalia curling her nose up "Careful not to breath it in as
as we might get permanently polluted by it."

Bethanor reached further over to analyse the contents of
the tank.

"Some kind of oil" he said with surprise "This thing
must be really old, we haven't used that since before the
2027 cataclysm! Woah!"

The boats started to pull away from the rocks. They were
already heading out towards the sea, pulled on by the
lapping waves.

"That wasn't quite the plan," said Inalia "How does this
thing work? Where's the levitation on it? It must be real-

ly heavy…"

The gang were scuttling around the boat like ants trying to understand their new environment when suddenly there was a "put, put, put…" sound and the motor died. The three looked at one another.

"I guess whoever it belongs to doesn't have an endless energy supply then," suggested Kalto

"Do you think it's been here since before 2027?" asked Inalia.

"No way!" said Bethanor "that would make it something like almost 70 years old!"

"It must belong to someone," said Inalia "and we probably should take it back."

"You know how to swim right?" laughed Kalto.

Inalia looked at him as if to say "*get real…*"

"Don't you have one of those Seasons tribe dresses that replicate fish aerodynamics when they come into contact with water? They look really cool," asked Kalto trying to sound helpful.

"As it happens I do," replied Inalia "I just don't have it with me."

"Shame," added Bethanor laughing under his breath "I guess we just swim the traditional way then."

"Swim?" Are you serious" added Inalia "There might be anything in this water. All kinds of toxic waste or weird evolved sea creatures, with like five heads. No way, not me...."

Inalia started to pull her Regster out of her pack. "Really," she said "You do like to complicate things don't you? Not ideal to launch from here but we can manage" she said confidently.

Kalto and Bethanor looked at one another.

"Well we can't stay here," added Bethanor "The tide is still moving us away from the land at a rate of 3 meters per second so the longer we wait, the more we're likely to need your special fish dress!"

"Can you compose a sort of rope from the metal tanks there?" Inalia asked as she span around to come to a halt at the front of the boat. "We can pull it back to shore."

The two friends flanked Inalia. "Lead the way Princess Inalia" Bethanor announced as they all headed towards the shore.

As they approached the shoreline, they noticed that the

other boat wasn't there anymore.

"I don't want to go back through the cave," said Inalia "It gives me the chills. Let's tie the boat further to the right down there in that cove," she said as she pointed to a nearby enclave. "Its not far," she encouraged.

"We can then manoeuvre up the side of the cliff face and back onto our track South," added Bethanor "Best not to hang around here."

The friends rested to find their bearings on the top of the cliff edge.

"What are we actually looking for?" Asked Kalto

"One of the researchers said there are populations of the toxic plants that are on the banks of a river 13 kilometres to the South. Should we take a look for ourselves?" asked Bethanor.

"Let's go," agreed Inalia.

"Anything to move away from this place," added Kalto

The wind had died down so they could make good progress as they veered inland. There was only desolate wasteland in all directions until, after around 10 minutes of heading South, the scenery opened out into miles of rocky canyons. Our friends descended lower and lower to where a river was ambling between the bends of the canyon at the very bottom. They followed the river's edge for several more minutes until some vegetation started to appear. More and more, winding and covering parts of the water, just as the researchers had described. A brown, rotting, tangled mass of vines stretched out across the river which was attempting, with much difficulty, to push past the putrid blockade. They signalled to one another to land on the left-hand bank of the river, not far from the vegetation. Their intention, to gain a deeper understanding of the surrounding environment and take some samples back with them.

"So here we are" announced Inalia almost triumphantly.

"And here they are," replied Bethanor storing his Regster and heading over towards the plants to get a better look.

Inalia and Kalto prepared sample boxes whilst Bethanor started to explore. The banks were rocky and fairly steep. He moved cautiously as he approached the river's edge, one step at a time, firming his footing each time. At the edge he sat for a moment contemplating the silent surroundings.

The white flowers looked almost surreal woven in between the tangles of ugly, brown vines. They were a prefect white, in the form of a lily. The whole area was covered with thousands of them. It actually looked like a beautiful contrast to the surrounding desolation and the brown-grey tinged water in which they were languishing. If they didn't suspect their role in deteriorating the Aurora Belt then they would once again have been filled with a sense of hope at seeing so many of them proliferate. Bethanor felt a sense of accomplishment as he sat there looking around. They had made it alone to this sector of New Earth. Everyone would certainly be proud of them bringing back more samples to work with. Now he felt they were really contributing to the work of the research group. This felt more like taking his place as part of the Sparks community rather than presenting some stupid project.

"Look at Eldregin's sculpture. Sure it's beautiful but it's just sitting in his garden," he thought "What use is that?" His grandfather was right, innovation is about making things better for everyone, lifting humanity. He could see that now.

He stood up again and looked ahead. There were rocks which appeared between the plants which would allow him to get some good samples. He proceeded towards a clump which was close to the side. Inalia approached with the boxes ready to receive the samples. She held them towards Bethanor as he eased out isolated pieces of the branches that had broken away along with some of the flowers.

"These look like they just broke away," said Inalia "They must have been caught by the current."

As he stepped out onto the third rock close to the clump, he felt it give way under his feet and in a split second he was falling backwards. Inalia launched forward to grab his arm in an attempt to catch him but his weight unbalanced her too and she found herself head first in the water. She gasped as she came up for air, tangled within the vines. The water was extremely cold and she called out to the others. Bethanor reached forward to take her arm, pulling at the vines to free her. She looked at him with panic in her eyes. She had been caught totally by surprise. In the next moment he was pulling her up onto the rocks once more with Kalto having arrived on the scene to help them. He hauled himself up behind her, dripping wet but looking proud of his rescue.

"Are you ok?" asked Inalia.

"Yes thanks," replied Bethanor as he held out two of the flowers that he had managed to keep hold of throughout the ordeal.

They were a little crumpled but they'd still be sufficient for research purposes. He smiled widely and Inalia hugged him in a spontaneous display of relief. He blushed and as Kalto noticed, he hurried the group on to finish their work there and Inalia sat for a moment to let the shock pass.

"We have no idea what is in that water," she said "It

could be extremely toxic like the plants".

She looked deeply into the pearls of waters that had collected on her clothes and were gently reflecting in the sun. There were indeed molecules that she didn't recognize.

"Bethanor, do you know what this molecule is?" she asked in a worried tone. He looked down at his own wet clothing.

"No," he said "Best that we head back to Reviathan quickly to clean ourselves up. It could be anything."

They gathered their packs, samples and supplies without a word but he air heavy with their thoughts about the fact that they could have been infected. As Bethanor was removing his Regster from his pack, the piece of Violet Enigma slipped out, unravelling from its protective wrapping. It came to a halt at his feet. He paused for a moment, as always magnetised by its beauty. But then he felt something strange. A distinct trembling movement in his clothes which then started to vibrate over his whole body. The water was reacting to the mineral. He watched in awe as the unidentifiable molecules started to separate out into a halo around him, almost frozen in space for a second and then explulsed into a pile of grey powder on the floor around him. Bethanor saw that, sure enough, the remaining water on his body was now clean.

"What just happened there?" asked Kalto who was standing close by and doing a double-take. "Did you see what I just saw? Did that purple crystal thing just check you over?"

"I guess it does appear to have regenerative properties, just like Ellianon said," Bethanor announced excitedly as Inalia and Kalto looked on in fascination.

"You try Inalia," Bethanor suggested, beckoning her closer to the Violet Enigma.

Her proximity to it created exactly the same reaction and she felt a wave of relief come over her that they wouldn't be contaminated.

"Wow that's something!" She concluded.

"Now we have plenty to share with the others. Wait till they hear about this!" encouraged Kalto "Let's go. I think we've seen plenty here!"

Meanwhile, Ellianon was making progress in his trip to the North. He had once again crossed paths with Yargen who was in convoy with a group of nomads at the foot of the mountains. In the evening they sat around a large camp fire, playing music and talking about life.

Stars are very philosophical and enjoy sharing their be-

liefs on most topics. Although quite impartial in con-
flicts, they have strong principles. Because of this, they
like to imagine how things 'can be' to the point sometimes of being quite opinionated if they want to make
themselves heard.

That evening, the atmosphere was relaxed and joyful.
People were busily making the final preparations for
meals that were to be shared, as always in gratefulness
for another day of freedom. The fire crackled softly in
the background as Ellianon explained the Enadon's vision to Yargen.

"Interesting indeed," the nomad replied, rubbing his chin
in deep thought. "This does sound very much like the
Tree of Justice," he agreed. "Its name comes from the
resolution of a deep injustice that a girl found herself in
with her family. Many centuries ago she was accused of
being a sorceress because of her very strong connection
to the forces of life. From a young age she knew the
names and properties of all of the plants and how they
could heal. She lived and breathed in tune with the cycles of nature and could feel the onset of natural disas-
ters. When she tried to warn people, at first they didn't
listen and then people began to talk about how strange
she was, her premonitions. In their fear, her family began
to turn against her. She was really just a Season Tribe
precursor, listening to what nature was telling her."

Yargen closed a pocket book he had been holding in his

lap and leaned forward to remove a rusting old kettle from the fire. He poured two cups of steaming herbal tea for his guest and himself. Cupping it between his hands to feel the warmth, he looked down at the surface of the tea, the ripples dispersing slowly.

"She prayed to nature to help her to find a solution," he continued "And one day a Star Triber named Ballentor returned to her time to speak with her. 'When you find your gifts normal and you accept them, so others will accept you too. Teach the ways of nature. Do not fear who you are or the power of what you know to be true' he told her. She set about showing small examples at first of how nature supported us, she healed her neighbours with her knowledge of herbs and taught them how to prepare tinctures that would prevent them becoming ill again. She decided to simply let everyone see who she really was and in doing so, as she grew she became a leader in her community. The story says that she named the Tree of Justice because she realised that what she had seen as unjust was simply a set of circumstances that forced her to stand up and be who she really was. Every day she lit a candle at the base of the tree to thank Ballentor for his wisdom and she spent the remainder of her life tirelessly serving her community and addressing anything which she saw upset their harmony with nature. A candle is still lit every day by the Season's tribe of the region."

"There are people still living in New Earth?" Enquired

Ellianon

"Oh yes, but not many," replied Yargen "Only those who truly believe so fully in the future regeneration of New Earth that they are willing to sacrifice all they have. You will find them at the encampment to the East of the Tree of Justice."

"Thank you my friend," Ellianon said, touching foreheads with Yargen as if to convey his innermost gratitude to him through his thoughts.

"May life continue to support you in your search my friend," replied Yargen. "We are all seekers," he concluded.

The music continued into the night and the Stars continued to share their stories. Ellianon woke the following day amongst the morning dew, ready to make headway that day through the mountains. As he was folding his last supplies into his pack, he was startled to hear the screech of the Enadon circling above him, and then elegantly swooping through the clouds to the North.

Ellianon smiled widely. "I guess you do want to help me too" he thought as he prepared himself psychologically for the track ahead. The wind was calm but icy as the sun once again fought without success to find a path through the dust and haziness of New Earth.

"Lead on dear Enadon!" Ellianon said as he started out, wrapping his cape close.

When it came to the mountains, Ellianon preferred to walk than to use a Regster. It was longer but more secure and in any case, he liked to study the environment as he passed. It would be easy to miss something intriguing if he just raced by. Being present to his surroundings also kept him alert and clear-headed. As he progressed, there was frequent rock-fall from the cliffs above that he had to dodge skilfully. The Enadon was calling from a way ahead. Ellianon could hear it faintly in the distance. The paths were narrow in this part of the region and he couldn't afford to let it distract him as he might slip.

As he approached a bend in the path, he could hear the sound echo deeper into a great hollow, so loudly that it felt to him like a huge hole in the Earth. Here were the remains of a huge landslide that had ripped away the side of the mountain ahead of him. Ellianon carefully removed his Regster.

"No choice here," he thought "Time to fly!"

He charged up and was soon soaring high above the mass of destruction below. Still no sign of life for as far as he could see. Then all of a sudden from his right, a flock of birds cut across his path, startling him. He zipped to one side and twisted in the air to avoid a collision, regaining his balance with some difficulty.

He took a split second decision to land for a moment in order to regain his composure. What he saw on the ground was the Tree of Justice in the distance. The area around it was surrounded by a hazy mist so it was barely recognisable but the magenta and green light that surrounded it was unmistakable. It was closer than he had thought and sure enough there was a lighted candle at its base.

Ellianon approached slowly. In the rocky hillside off to the right he could make out the shapes of three figures who were sitting in a circle. He decided to approach them first as a mark of respect. They were animatedly discussing the story of the two Star Youngers who had broken the laws of time jumping in order to see each other again. This seemed to be quite a point of contention within the Reviathan community and even within this remote group of Seasons about how the matter should have been dealt with by the Stars. Ellianon could hear the huffs of dissatisfaction between the flow of conversation. Then one man turned towards him. He must have been startled by his footsteps as he approached. Few people visited these parts.

Ellianon greeted them with a nod of respect and stretched out his five fingers to meet theirs. Their looks of surprise softened to peaceful expressions of welcome and they made a place for him by the fire. He introduced the reason for his quest and his audience listened with intent. As Seasons, they knew both the ways of nature and the surrounding environment with amazing precision. The elder of the three men looked down and stirred his tea with a sense of reflection.

"If your need is really for repairing the Earth then there is no question that we will help you," he replied calmly.

"Why do you call it F563? This does not sound like a name given by nature herself?" he asked Ellianon jokingly.

"It is a material that is partially validated by the Spark laboratories. Let's say it has a nickname," Ellianon smiled.

There was plenty of F563 in the nearby mine they told Ellianon and they would be happy to guide him there. He gratefully accepted and they were soon on their way.

Soon enough they were standing at the entrance which had unfortunately been covered by a layering of rockfall. Ellianon stepped forward lifting his hands openly towards the rocks which started immediately to vibrate and then to explode into tiny fragments of spinning molecules. He shifted the swirling mass to an empty space just to the right.

"After you," he indicated to the Seasons with a proud smile.

Ellianon held his torch high in front of him to light the way. The Seasons were of course capable of seeing in the dark. Their pupils transformed to resemble a cat's.

The passages were tight and the air was cold and heavy as it lingered in the dark. They walked what felt like 200 metres and suddenly there it was. Piled high in the centre of the junction of four adjacent mine shafts, an abundance of F563. Its blue sheen was unmistakable. Ellianon moved closer to investigate. Excellent! It was mostly pure, but some had elements of calcite which would not be a problem to remove. Once again he used his powers to move about twenty five rocks onto a small cart that was waiting nearby on a set of tracks. One of the Seasons tribesmen operated a lever to send it rumbling to the surface.

At the nearby village, a Star nomad was resting and watering his herd with a group of Season locals. Ellianon traded a yak with him and the Seasons helped him to secure the stones. He decided to make a stop at the Tree of Justice and himself lit a candle in thanks for the help he received, this time from the Seasons. An elder who had followed him to the sacred space, reached out to hold his hands in his own. He looked deeply and reverently into Ellianon's eyes and said "A hui hou", see you soon in Hawaiian. "A'ohe Hana Nui Ka Alu'ia". Remember, no task is too big when done together. He nodded in respect, thanked the old man and was soon making his final preparations for the long return journey back to Reviathan.

As Friday's meeting approached, Bethanor's excitement grew. The night before, he lay awake thinking about all of the directions that the research could take now that they had seen the plants in their natural environment. He could not help wondering why they were there in the first place? They had only been documented for the first time on Earth around 80 years ago, a hybrid of an orchid and a species of orange blossom (Neroli) which at some point became wild, spreading fervently and causing havoc. Instead of emitting healing properties as Neroli oil was said to do since the ancient Egyptians used it to heal their minds, bodies and spirits, these plants were turning against their environment like a cancer. What was not in balance? He thought about what Inalia had said about the dangers of affecting the natural balance of life with genetic hybrids. This could well be an example, a catastrophic one. They'd seen it first-hand and they had plenty of samples to share now.

The Committee would surely be delighted at the progress that they have made if he explained carefully how the research had been carried out" Bethanor mused. What if he wrote a summary for the Committee before the meeting to keep them informed of their progress?

"They would be more receptive and perhaps provide

them with support," he thought.

He rolled the arguments over and over in his mind, occasionally reaching for his Messagepad to note an important element. It was 2 a.m. and all was quiet outside. Only the sound of the wind gently tapping at the window of his quarters. Since he was awake, he might as well write the memo now. No time like the present and he couldn't sleep anyway. It would be ready to send after their meeting with the Eastern Suburbs in the morning. He rose from his bed and meandered to the kitchen to get something to drink and some nourishment, motivating what was going to be a long night. He felt a sense of purpose as he pulled two peaches and a small bunch of grapes from the permaculture box above the main table. He found courage with each positive thought he brought to mind, "Yes they would convince them, they would find a way to make everyone's research visible, he would not let the team down."

He returned to his desk to set about his task. He took a deep breath and he started to write. The context of how the question of the toxic plants came about, the hypotheses they were working with, what had already been researched in the past and why they were excluding that from their research to follow a new branch of analysis, and finally the samples and data that they had collected until now. He included each member of the team, everyone that had even contributed an idea. He exposed all of the sources of data they had used. Page after page of explanations flowed from his train of thought until, at 3.46 am, he placed his heavy head down on his folded arms and fell asleep. The screen in front of him blinked gently, showing diagrams of connections found between different possible solutions, like a giant subway map.

Bethanor woke with a start. His messagepad was making a resounding noise as it became clear that Inalia was trying to contact him.

"Where are you?" she asked sharply. "The call with the Eastern Suburbs is supposed to start in five minutes!"

Bethanor looked at the time, startled. He had more than over-slept and now he'd have to hurry to be on time to support the very people he didn't want to let down. How ironic was that! As he pulled on some clothes and headed over to the hide-out, the presentation he'd written the night before whirred in his mind.

"Had he covered everything? What if he missed a vital step?" he caught himself building up these worries into an unnecessary drama and concentrated back on this morning's meeting.

Inalia had already started the meeting as he walked through the door and was sharing their samples from New Earth. All was well and she was handling everything smoothly. He couldn't help feeling a little guilty but at the same time he also felt a sense of pride at seeing her managing the whole arrangements calmly. He re-membered how nervous she'd felt in the beginning. He looked deeply at her for a moment, feeling a sense of overwhelming connection with her, like time paused for a split-second. He hurried over to apologise for his ab-sence.

The conversation quickly moved on to the important questions : What effect was the Violet Enigma having on the water by removing the grey matter and could it also affect the plants? What to do with the grey matter so its not volatile? Castedon was deep in thought. He was well aware of the approaching Committee meeting. Their time was running out yet he didn't quite see everything con-verging enough for them to have a proper case to present. There were kilometres and kilometres of these toxic plants to treat. How could they possibly apply a solution to all of them? The Sparks weren't allowed to modify living organisms. The clean-up would perhaps also need the help of the Seasons Tribe.

"What if we enlist the help of the Streams?" someone asked from the back of the meeting room in the Eastern Suburbs. "With their abilities to move water, they could help us to partition the river to separate the top layer and channel it off into a separate tank or confined section. It would then be of sufficiently small volume that we could decompose it into the different elements, removing whatever the grey powder is that the Violet Enigma didn't like."

"It would break up the stagnancy which seems to be allowing the plants to proliferate in the first place," added another researcher "Let's see how they grow in clean water."

"I like it!" said Kalto. Inalia was diligently taking notes at this stage as Bethanor took over chairing the meeting for a moment. He was drawing out a schema on the co-lab screen.

"What do we do with the grey powder that's removed when we decompose? It might be volatile? We don't know what it is yet."

"Yes, it most certainly will be volatile," agreed one of the researchers. "It will need to be disposed of carefully so as not to contaminate New Earth in another way."

"What if we combine it with F563?" Suggested another researcher wearing a green cloak "the effect would be to neutralise its acidity."

"And we could maybe even then use it to fertilise the surrounding environment if our calculations are correct?"

"So let me recap," said Inalia "(1) We ask the streams for help in partitioning the contaminated water of the rivers which we channel into water tanks we've prepared (2) The grey matter is filtered out and quarantined just like the Violet Enigmas showed us, ready to perform further tests (3) If the rivers start to flow again, the plants might not be able to spread so easily, and (4) We potentially combine with F563 to neutralise the grey matter. Deeper analysis is needed there to ensure it's a safe solution and see if it can be used to fertilise the surrounding area..... Did I miss anything?"

"I have a really strong intuition that it will work," said the researcher with the green cloak clearly finding it difficult to contain his excitement. "I've been studying the fusion properties of F563 for some time now. I can show you."

He opened a silver metallic case containing four glass vials, lifting out one containing a sample of the plant and another which was labelled F563. Its contents looked like three tiny crystals with a blue hue. Kalto immediately recognised them as the element that the Enadon had shown to them on the way to the Eastern Suburbs.

"That's it!" he blurted out "That's the material from the vision we saw. It could well be the right direction! Where did you find this F563?"

"It was given to me by a nomad I met some weeks ago," replied the researcher. "I was looking for a new angle for my research and it just so happened that I helped this person out of a tricky situation and this is the gift that he generously gave to me. He told me that he had brought it back from his last voyage as he had been captivated by its beautiful blue hue. He found that it a inspired a sense of peacefulness. There was just something about it that made him feel safe. It's true that I often felt calmer when I was working in it's vicinity. Watch..."

He beckoned people forward with an enthusiastic sweep of the hand.

He reached into the vial with a pair of longer tongs and pulled out a crystal which probably measured just two centimetres in breadth. He placed it gently on a square of clear plastic so everyone could see it and then proceeded to pick up some of the grey substance which he placed in the palm of his hand. He closed his eyes to concentrate. As he opened them, he could see the small crowd of people around him eagerly fixated on what was going to happen, hoping that the fusion would work. He raised his hand in front of his line of vision and then, scooping up the crystal, he brought his two hands together cupping the two elements together. As he looked intensely at the elements, they began to oscillate, faster and faster. The blue colour became stronger and spiralled in a haze between the other molecules of the dullish grey toxic remnants. Sparks of white light projected from the fusion as always and the oscillation slowed. Within his hands, the green-caped researcher now held a piece of chalky blue rock.

The resulting specimen was handed from person to person, each one inspecting the result with more or less depth. The room was in quiet contemplation of the result. You could see that they were all integrating the new data. F563 was an unclassified element. It had not been analysed fully by scientists and this was the first time that most people had seen it. The green-caped researcher was checking some measures against his previous tests when another researcher broke the silence.

"It does seem plausible, pretty inoffensive," he stated turning it gently in his line of sight.

"The Committee have come across this element before, it's just that their research has not been very in-depth. It's quite rare to find it. I believe it comes from somewhere in the North-Western Emeria region. A very arid and inhospitable place."

"That's right," said Ellianon entering the room with a triumphant smile. "I know exactly where that is now, and I've brought 6 kilos of it with me. That should be enough to start us off."

"Sounds like a plan," enthused Castedon, welcoming his friend back with a wide smile and a traditional five finger touch.

A third researcher was busily scribbling on his notebook.

"Calculating the area of land mass and the volume we

can decompose at any one time, at this rate it would take us 16 months to complete this decomposition work, assuming that there are six of us working intensively," he added in a concerned voice "the tear in the atmosphere is growing at a rate of 2mm per day so this means that during that time it is likely to have grown by 97.3 cm assuming a worst case scenario that it doesn't slow at all during the time we're treating the plants. Can we afford to wait that long?"

Everyone in the room paused and looked at each other. They knew that this meant many cubic metres of rayadon gas still filling the atmosphere.

"We can recruit more help," said Bethanor positively. "The committee will help us."

"At least we have a potential solution," smiled Castedon "We are one step further ahead than we were yesterday!"

The grand day of the Committee meeting arrived. Bethanor had prepared his speech with precision. The research group had reached a clear, collective view about what the solution was and how it would be carried out so he was feeling confident. It would be safe to say that he was also proud of how they had all pulled together to contribute to the solution they were proposing. Even better was the fact that it was based on the Eastern and Western Suburbs working together. Outside the great oak-panelled doors Bethanor could be heard from many meters away pacing along the corridor. He recited to himself in harmony with his steps. His arguments were clear, one, hypothesis, two, analysis, three, solution, four, implementing the solution. It helped to calm his nerves to walk and breathe deeply. His mother, Kalto and Inalia were sitting at a row of seats to his left, talking quietly but with an obvious sense of excitement in their voices.

At 3.30pm the doors creaked widely open and a man stepped out through them.

"Be welcome" he offered holding his five fingers aloft.

Bethanor reached forward to greet him as the others rose to their feet and prepared to file into the room behind him.

A soft-spoken woman rose from a chair on the far side of the room.

"Welcome Zenalis and Bethanor, welcome Inalia and Kalto," she said. "We are honoured by your presence with us today". She beckoned and everyone sat in a circle, a little anxiety now filling the air.

"Bethanor, we read your request for presence before us here today and the analysis that you sent for the attention of the committee concerning the delegation exploring the degradation of the Aurora Belt. Would you like to explain the context of this request to speak with us?" She placed the Messagepad down in front of her. She and two other men looked patiently at Bethanor who was preparing himself to speak. The room was silent. Bethanor cleared his throat and shifted from one foot to another slightly nervously. He could feel his palms starting to sweat and he inadvertently crumpled the edge of his notes moving them into his other hand.

"So," he started "I asked to speak to you because the situation with the Aurora Belt is becoming critical and I have a strong conviction that we can stop it, or at least reverse some of the continuing damage."

"Go on," she offered.

"We have seen that the Belt is impacted particularly negatively by the increasing amount of the toxic gas rayadon. This gas is emitted by hybrid plants that are found to be proliferating in parts of the New Earth region. We believe their increasing volume to be causing a good proportion of the impact on the tear in the atmosphere." Bethanor continued with the hypothesis, outlining the different aspects that had been raised during the previous preparation meeting.

All was going smoothly and he felt more and more confident explaining out the outcomes of the communal work. He arrived at the solution and the Committee continued to smile benevolently until, no, there it was…the moment of difficulty…he said it…we propose to combine the toxic grey residue with F563. He watched the colour drain as if in slow motion from the faces of the Committee members.

One of the men paused him to clarify. "Did you say F563? Did we hear correctly?" he questioned.

"Yes," replied Bethanor "But it has been tested, we took no risks." Zenalis looked shocked but refrained from intervening. She knew what the Committee would say. And they waited no longer to share their concern.

"Bethanor, F563 is an unvalidated element, we should not be discussing this. I hope you are not incorporating this element seriously into your work and using an element which is unauthorised? I believe you know that this element is prohibited?"

"But many of the researchers agree on its potential as a neutralising molecule. We're confident this will work!"

The Committee fell silent, as if inviting a moment of realisation for everyone in the room. The presentation was going no further. Zenalis was also reflective. She was saddened for Bethanor, having his hopes dashed but at the same time the rules were clear and they had discussed tampering with unvalidated elements so part of her was also disappointed. Even though Bethanor wasn't decomposing F563 himself, he was clearly collaborating with people who were. Her heart sank.

Bethanor couldn't understand the wall of rigidity that he was suddenly confronted with and the perceived injustice of it all left him feeling very angry.

"Don't you care that the tear is getting worse? Isn't that more important than some stupid rule?" he stated loudly, his body trembling with frustration.

"We need a framework to live by Bethanor, otherwise our creations would lead to chaos. We have seen the devastation that people can bring when they create without properly thinking through the impact on others" said the lady from the Committee. "We understand your frustration and we thank you for your concern for solving this problem for your community. We understand that your intentions were good". She looked at him benevolently "When F563 is validated we can look at this possibility more deeply and you can even be part of the research team since you will have come of age by then."

"The tear will grow another 98 centimeters within the next year!" he retorqued.

There was another pause. "Bethanor, the best we can do is to make this validation a higher priority in the Committee's agenda" they replied.

"That would be a good start" said Bethanor arrogantly.

He thanked them for their time although the resentment was clear in his voice, and he paced out of the room stopping just outside to breathe in a large lung full of air. as Inalia and Kalto joined him he was shaking his head in disbelief.

"Procedures!" he scolded "The Committee and their damn lists!"

Just as he started to pace furiously up and down, Kalto saw two figures arriving in the distance. Their outlines growing bigger and bigger until he recognised them as Ellianon and Castedon. What were they doing here? They rarely came to these parts of Reviathan.

As soon as they caught up with their friends, Castedon and Ellianon could see that things hadn't gone well. They could see the disappointment on their faces and Bethanor fell silent, hanging his head slightly.

"You have let noone down Bethanor," said Castedon "This was never going to be an easy conversation," and with that, he headed towards the wooden doors and disappeared out of view. Ellianon patted each of them on the back and followed Castedon inside. Zenalis was still inside discussing with the Committee whom she knew well. As she turned to see who was joining them, expecting to see Bethanor return, the surprise was evident on her face.

"Castedon?" she said.

"Hello my dear sister," he replied "It has been a while."

"Twenty years," she replied without needing to reflect, almost nostalgically. "What are you doing here? Are you part of the research team? Then I see you have met Bethanor…"

"Yes, he's a marvellous young man. I had no idea he was your son. I guess I can see the similarities now," he replied with a nod of acknowledgement.

By this time, Bethanor and friends had opened the main door slightly to listen in. Kalto and Inalia looked at Bethanor who was once again absorbing the revelation.

"Castedon is my uncle?" he whispered to them, his eyes wide with surprise.

"What a surprise," said one of the Committee members "It has indeed been a while Castedon and I see you are still condoning the use of dubious methods for your innovations."

Castedon did not react to the cristicism. He simply smiled calmly at the man then started to speak.

"The teams have worked to the standards employed by the Committee to bring their research this far. Many are ex-Committee researchers as you know."

"Yes and they left the Committee research teams," interrupted the man bluntly.

"But that does not mean that the quality of their work decreased or that they are different people," replied Castedon. "You create what you see as two different systems because of your own 'us versus them' mentality. You label us rebels and recluses simply because we do not agree with your methods and will not sacrifice our creative ideals. Labels reduce and segregate people when we are really all the same flesh and blood."

The tension in the room transformed into an awkward silence. Everyone knew that this was true. After a moment, the lady broke the silence.

"You are right dear Castedon, yet the rules are here to protect us all and you choose not to live by them. And can we deduce that you are also encouraging others to do so?"

Bethanor burst into the room, in defence of Castedon. "We asked for his help!" he blurted out.

"Then perhaps you should have asked for your mother's first," recommended the third man. She is a most distinguished innovator who abides by the framework to achieve remarkable results." Zenalis smiled gently but was still showing concern with the direction of the discussions.

"My son, I understand how you wish to explore and innovate deeply but humankind created so many monstrosities in the past by only thinking of selfish, personal gains. Many did not pay attention to the impact of their work on others and the best use of the resources we have to support us all. Look where it got us, to the point of an ecological cataclysm. How do we avoid this again if we don't maintain some guidelines that people choose to respect? Every element needs to prove its stability before being freely available."

Bethanor was infuriated by the injustice "Then if I prove that it is stable you will let us use it? You will give this plan a chance?" he asked defiantly.

"We would all be fools not to," interjected Ellianon. "I have seen so much of the devastation with my own eyes. If Reviathan was to become like New Earth then we will not survive either, rules or no rules!"

The leader of the Committee looked aside for a moment as if looking for inspiration. The atmosphere in the room was filled with a sense of disappointment. She took a deep breath, rubbed her forehead and looked around at each person in front of her.

"So be it," replied the lady. "Our objective here is not to

change the rules but to ensure that this environmental problem is dealt with as a top priority. We can afford a few days more, rather than increase the risks. We will convene here when your research is complete Bethanor and we propose that you work under the safe conditions of the Committee research unit, with Fenrick's team. He will rearrange his schedule for us to test the F563."

"Thank you," replied Bethanor "So be it."

Chapter Eight

The Aurora Belt

The following morning Bethanor found himself climbing the stairs towards the research labs. The high, glass ceilings and floors let in an enormous amount of light which filled the main entrance with much clarity and optimism. The whole place had been designed to let a maximum of natural light fill the space. Bethanor could see many people on different floors moving precisely and diligently about their activities. Discussions were underway, co-lab screens with sketches and holographic designs were scattered all over the place. Some people were communicating remotely via the new Auric screens that are held up by a wire that either wraps around your ear, into which there's a small speaker, or plaits into your hair so you don't have to hold them. Bethanor had seen them once or twice out in the streets. They are so light that they appear to float.

The hub was alive with exchange, much like the Eastern Suburbs only surrounded by more formal white and silver chairs and tables. Everything looked pristine and sparkling clean.

"A clear environment is fundamental to maintaining a clear mind," said a voice behind him. Fenrick was here to welcome him. "Let me show you around!" He said heartily as he patted Bethanor on the back.

The corridors were wide, leaving space for people to stop and discuss at any moment. There were other areas with all kinds of displays of materials, floor to ceiling tubes within which the materials could be securely transported and reinforced glass boxes into which the researchers could insert their hands to fuse or decompose without it affecting anything in the room. There was a distinct yet subtle smell of smoke which Bethanor recognised as coming from the combustion process. There were people sitting with co-pads discussing what looked like a complex topic. They were pulling in data from the Alpha Light Network to reinforce what they were saying. As they spoke, the data zoomed in highlighting the appropriate portions of text in purple so everyone could verify the exactness of the innovation or molecule that was being analysed. Animated conversation and body language filled the building with a buzz of enthusiasm.

The two filed through the areas, Bethanor even more in awe with each room and with each person who was presented to him. "Here we are. Room K75" said Fenrick looking into the retina-activated security which set the sliding door opening widely. "We'll have you set up for that in no time" Fenrick reassured. In front of him two women and a man smiled widely, each reaching forward to welcome him. After the tension of the Committee meeting the day before, Bethanor was a little surprised by the warm welcome he was receiving. As he glanced to his left, he was surprised to see another figure, Castedon waiting patiently in the corner of the room.

"This is Mariena, Enarom and Renelle," introduced Fenrick. Each stepped forward to touch fingers one after the other, looking at Bethanor with a certain mix of benevolence and anticipation.

Castedon crossed the room to greet them. Bethanor looked inquisitively at him. "This is more important than differences of opinion," he said firmly.

"Castedon knows this research case well and we are lucky to have him here to work with us," said Fenrick "and we have no time to lose if I understood correctly? Perhaps you would like to brief us on your research so far Bethanor?"

The people in the room looked at him eagerly. One opened a Co-Lab screen and brought up the notes that Kalto had been adding over the past weeks.

"We've been following your work closely," he said.

Everyone sat as Bethanor took a deep breath and lunged into his explanation in the minutest detail. Minutes and hours passed as questions were asked amid all of the discussions, diagrams and data. Castedon added remarks at different moments here and there to solidify the arguments and reinforce details of the research process that

Bethanor had not seen since he hadn't been in the Eastern Suburbs with them.

"I feel that the next step is to work backwards from your findings on combining F563 with the grey matter to determine at what point it becomes stable and what molecule needs to be neutralised within the grey matter."

"We have received more samples of F563 from Ellianon who arrived yesterday with Castedon so we can work under excellent conditions," reassured Enarom. "They are all stored in the un-validated materials sector as the code requires but we can recover them as needed."

"Then let us get to work," enthused Renelle "What order?"

"I propose that we also separate the F563 into its numerous components and test the reaction of each sub-component with the grey matter, see where that leads us," suggested Mariena.

"Sounds like a plan," said Castedon with his usual high dose of positivity. "Ok for everyone?"

There were nods of agreement from each person, sending everyone into action managing their own specialised part of the preparation for the deep analysis of F563. The room soon became busy with creating samples, fusion of elements and storing of research data. Analysis of the results would wait for the following morning when the number of tests was sufficiently interesting to make it credible.

At the end of his first day Bethanor was exhausted but felt the need to see his two closest friends on the way home. They arranged to meet at the hideout where Kalto was already waiting for his friend, a large glass of dragonfruit juice in hand for him. He and Inalia were waiting for a recount of the day.

Bethanor shared all of the team's progress. They had worked really hard, being careful also to ensure that the conditions under which they worked were absolutely thorough so that nothing in their results could be questioned.

Inalia was happy that the progress were promising but at the same time rather envious that she had not been invited to participate. It seemed like all the excitement was going on without her. She asked lots of questions and made suggestions so that she could still feel involved. She could see that Bethanor was sensitive to her feeling excluded. He explained what was happening in the minutest detail and they discussed her suggestions intently. This made her feel even closer to him. She could tell that he cared. Kalto didn't appear so attentive to the recount of the day. He was busy folding a napkin into an origami bird. "One day I'll fly away…." He sang to himself in a voice that mimicked a singer from before the cataclysm.

He was making wild gestures in the air as if to send it lovingly on its way "fly birdie, fly..." he wafted the paper 30 centimetres out in front of him and watched as it nose-dived rapidly to make an emergency landing on the floor below with Kalto standing above looking perplexed. Inalia didn't mind Kalto's antics, they meant that she had all of Bethanor's attention, even if she wasn't intending to make it clear that it was so important to her. They could talk for as long as they wanted whilst Kalto occupied himself with his comic scenarios.

As the explanations came to an end, Bethanor and Inalia felt very inspired. What if it really worked? Would there really be no more radiation to impact the tear in the atmosphere? Tomorrow was another dense day of research tests so the friends parted ways as the sun was setting, Bethanor once again promising to share the team's work at the end of the day.

As Bethanor arrived home he was welcomed as usual by his mother, open arms and also hungry for details of his day. He took a ripened pear from the permaculture box and sat down beside her in the kitchen to recount a shortened version this time, but ensuring to share the key details.

"I'm so very proud of you Bethanor," she said in a gentle voice. "It is important to keep our principles but also respect those of other people. The team told me how dedicated and diligent you were today with all the research.

How you cooperated and shared all that you had discovered in such a transparent and honest way." Bethanor blushed slightly.

"I learnt a lot from them," he replied "and Castedon was there to help too." Zenalis looked knowingly.

"Why didn't you tell me that he was my uncle?" Bethanor asked, trying to hide his feelings of hurt.

"Castedon made his choices and I respect them," she said "And I knew that if I told you of his whereabouts you would have wanted to go to the Eastern Suburbs. I expect that you would have been quite taken by the animation there. You always have been quite an explorer and a bit of a rebel." She smiled widely and Bethanor laughed at being understood so clearly.

"But as Sparks, we cannot continue to live in such a separate way can we?" he asked.

"We are creating a new world Bethanor we can agree on whatever rules we want collectively. Afterwards we must accept the consequences of the rules and choices we make. This is what it means to evolve to not go back to the unconscious ways of the 'Ostrich Syndrome'. I believe we can find a way but it is not always so easy." As she spoke, Zenalis picked up a nearby apple and a peach. Forming a spiral of elements and colours in her hands she proceeded to create a multi-coloured fruit which was a combination of the two.

"We can find balance and enjoyment in a new combination, but both have to accept to change, to give up their old identity to become something greater. Do you see?" she explained.

Bethanor nodded and quietly said goodnight to his mother. He laid in bed for a while watching the shadows dance across the windows and the stars through the panels above him. He thought about how far they had come in their adventure, how everything had fallen into place despite a few mishaps here and there. Sometimes it felt almost surreal. Then he remembered his project. The rite of passage was in only 6 days time and he hadn't progressed since testing the Chromavelia.

"Oh well, first thing's first. The research was far more important," he told himself as his eyes became heavy.

The following morning, Renelle was waiting for him in the research lab, making preparations for the new round of tests. Enthusiastic as ever she wanted to make the most of the whole day to progress their analysis. She smiled widely as she saw Bethanor arrive. He was taken aback by the dedication and openness of his new team. He felt blessed by this unexpected opportunity and so he quickly settled to prepare a plan for the day. One by one the rest of the team arrived not long afterwards, adding more and more vibrant anticipation to the room. Sparks just love to innovate and the ideas flowed easily within this environment of trust and with all the equipment they could possibly need.

Today, the molecules of the grey matter would be separated little by little to test its stability. The light shone through the window onto the F563 which sent rays of light blue light across the room. Just being in the presence of this energy gave the room a sense of peace. Bethanor looked deeply into the refracted light rays. They scintillated gently in the reflections on the white furniture of the room. He was captivated for a moment by its simple beauty. He took a rather large piece that was positioned close by and lifted it to his line of sight, looking deeply into its composition. Slowly, other members of the team stopped what they were doing and came closer to look too. This was the first time that they had seen F563 but it's properties were surrounded by myths of deep healing potential. Bethanor started to break away elements of the crystal, decomposing it slowly so everyone could witness the decomposition process.

"There, you see it?" cried Castedon a few moments later. "Now....at approximately 0.74 seconds of diffusion the gas is integrated, it switches state at that moment to become unstable. You can see the molecules vibrating wildly!" Reverse the process Bethanor, we'll time the re-fusion."

Bethanor took a deep breath to steady himself and then

concentrated hard. He could feel the suspense filling the room and it made him feel slightly nervous. "Take your time" reassured Renelle "we can do this as many times as we need to". Sure enough there it was, the gas was dispersed and the crystal stabilised beaming its blue rays around the room as if in celebration. The team was speechless, taking in the magic of the moment.

"That's it, that's the key. So the F563 is unstable because of the presence of this gas. It becomes a neutraliser when we remove it," said Fenrick calmly "I think we have something. I suggest we fuse this stage of the F563 generation with the grey matter. Now on to studying the grey matter. I propose that we decompose the grey matter, checking simultaneously its interaction with the F563."

There were echoes of agreement around the room. Enarom quickly prepared two samples and the team once again gathered together to see the process through. As Fenrick slowly combined the two samples, white sparks pulsing between blue, green and grey swirls, there were gasps of wonder. The room was flooded with the most amazing light any of them had ever experienced. They stood motionless and in silence, watching as the new material formed a pile of bluish-grey matter which resembled a crumbling crystal, similar to chalk.

"We have it," Castedon said finally, nodding slowly and still taking in the scene they had just witnessed.

Fenrick nodded. "I believe we do," he replied with a smile.

Many years of research had finally revealed a solution that might just have an impact of the Aurora Belt. Our team were taking in the awe of this realisation, and none more so than Bethanor whose eyes were wide with hope.

Recordings were made, the samples were quarantined and data filed within the Alpha Light Network to share their findings publicly. Everyone felt proud of their diligent work, but they now had to ensure that the stability of F563 could be demonstrated to the Committee in order for the results to be accepted. They each understood the importance of getting this stage right. After three more tests to ensure that the outcome was credible, they sent word immediately to the Committee to prepare an audience. They must progress with these promising results as soon as possible.

The Committee received them with quiet anticipation. Bethanor was invited to speak.

"We saw during our decompositions that at 0.56 seconds the grey matter can become neutralized because of the inherent stabilising properties of the F563. The two must be combined to let the F563 have its effect on the instable molecules of the grey matter. Together, the frequency of their vibrations lower as the F563 and the grey matter solidify to become what we are calling Halpion. We believe according to our calculations that this new element will have a stabilising and healing effect on the land around the banks of the river, and the plants which inhabit the area, causing them to reverse their expulsion of toxic gases. Based on these results, we ask for your validation to integrate both F563 and the new Halpion element into the official global Molecular Register of materials. We would also like to further our tests on the plants themselves."

The Committee had been listening intently and nodding as Bethanor spoke to demonstrate that they were following his analysis closely. They convened for a few moments to discuss the findings and any risks they could foresee. Bethanor felt a flush of cold sweat and slightly nauseous as he waited for their verdict. The head of the Committee finally turned and called for attention.

"Following the experiments that have been carried out and Bethanor's testimonial of the promising results, along with a clear demonstration of the stable capacities of the F563, we validate the continued use of these elements in our search for a solution to the atmospheric tear in the Aurora Belt. Excellent work. You may continue with access to all the resources you require and with our blessing."

The room filled with excitement and Bethanor felt a sigh of relief mixed with an amazing sense of satisfaction. They had done it. The solution looked highly promising.

He had done it. He'd presented their arguments and results with clarify and conviction, just as he'd imagined.

"Bethanor, you have shown us that you are a capable innovator, both inspiring others into action and respecting our responsibilities to one another to avoid unnecessary risks. We commend you for your perseverance. We'd like to offer you a permanent place with Fenrick's research team should you wish to continue investigating this and other issues together."

Bethanor felt himself blush with embarrassment, even if he generally liked being the centre of attention. Today he had only been thinking about solving the problem but it felt good to be recognised for his efforts. But what about Inalia and Kalto? He had been representing the group's work.

"I'd be really happy to join Fenrick," he replied with a smile "I think we can do a lot together" he replied. "But the work wasn't all mine" he concluded "It was Inalia's idea to start with."

"Then they are also welcome to contribute to the team's work," said the committee member, delighted that Bethanor was recognising everyone's part in co-creating a solution. "I think you are perhaps ready for your rite of passage," she added with a benevolent smile.

Several days later, in the quietness of a sunrise over New

Earth, the team gathered at the same water's edge. The light was slowly chasing away the night shadow to reveal dew drops and hues of pale orange across the nearby vegetation. The area looked like a silent painting of serenity yet as the light spread its net wider and wider, it revealed more and more patches of putrid, stagnant water and devastating black lesions on the surrounding vegetation. In the middle of this scene, the white flowers sat calmly, almost with an air of innocence about them.

"Who would have thought that they cause so much devastation?" Inalia whispered to Bethanor as they approached.

"It's always the pretty ones that are the most dangerous," replied Kalto laughing to himself. Bethanor laughed too, looking at Inalia as he did so. She responded with a small huff of indignation.

"Of course," she said sarcastically "Let's just get on with this shall we? We have lots to do rather than monkeying around this morning."

Then she smiled at her friends, feeling grateful that they were part of such a momentous event. Her blond hair was shining radiantly in the morning sun and Bethanor once again felt a rush of admiration for his friend.

There were Season and Stream tribe members gathered there with them, just as they had imagined. The Tribes standing side by side to work on testing if the solution would really work. The scene was extremely inspiring. The tanks were placed, ready to receive the water and the Streams prepared themselves to do their part to channel the water into them. Fenrick paused everyone to share a few words.

"This morning, my heart fills with much hope that we may find a solution, but also much pride to see our fellow tribesmen here with us today. We thank you our friends for your time and your trust in collaborating with us. I pray that Reviathan will today be healed once more, but in whatever outcome, I am once again honoured to work with you all."

With that, the water in front of them started to ripple, then to oscillate. People watched with enthusiasm as small peaks of waves started to appear. The Streams were standing proudly and solidly in a line across the shallow river, their hands stretched out in front of them, palms raised to the sky. They sang in unison, a way of giving thanks to the universe for allowing their gift to work for the good of all. Currents were forming here and there as they used their hands to gently form wafting movements in the air. One of the Streams signalled to the others who proceeded to raise their left hands higher than their right. Their left remained raised to the sky, whilst the right continued to waft in fluid motion. As they did so, the river parted creating two levels, one above the other. The lower level was running vigorously whilst the higher level remained stagnant. The grey, thickness of the toxicity was evident in the higher level. It was quite a sight for the Seasons and Sparks who were watching from the river banks. With a flick of their left hands, the Streams redirected the flow of the higher level into the awaiting tanks. They continued for what felt like an eternity to Inalia who was excitedly waiting to see the results.

Slowly but surely, as the minutes passed, the higher level became clearer and clearer, less and less, as water from higher up in the river began to emerge and run its natural course. The tanks filled up with a think sludge of the grey matter. The entanglements of vines and flowers started to bob gently up and down as the current passed. The Streams lowered their hands, allowing the river to continue to flow alone.

The Stream tribe members filed out of the water one by one, each of them exposed to the Violet Enigma, as Bethanor and Inalia had been, to ensure that they were properly decontaminated. They were greeted and thanked warmly by the rest of the group.

They all formed a circle and the Chief of the Seasons Tribe once again thanked nature for her support in rebalancing the environment here. The air was filled with a gentle sense of peaceful harmony as everyone stood together in gratitude.

Only moments later, the Sparks were busily preparing the samples of F563 to be used as neutralisers. The boxes were opened and slowly the crystals were lowered into the tanks at strategically calculated placements. Four Spark tribe members then stood at the corners of each of the tanks, ready to perform the fusion process. Inalia, Kalto and Bethanor were all assigned to the same tank. They smiled encouragingly at one another.

The tribespeople all took a deep breath in unison and leaned in to touch the surface of the grey sludge. They would have to concentrate hard since a sandstorm was starting to pick up. Fenrick gave a signal to the group and they commenced their fusion. The air around them filled with an enormous halo of white and blue light as the Sparks merged the two materials. The effect was astounding, far brighter than they had seen it in the laboratory. The matter swirled and sparked until it finally bonded into the same grey-blue chalky mass that their research had demonstrated.

Next was the turn of the Seasons Tribespeople who would distribute the Halpion in order to fertilise and regenerate the land. They had no idea how long this might take. They had prepared long furrows in a succession of parallel lines into which they were gently folding the chalk-like mineral, then closing over the surface with the remaining earth. This part of the plan would take a good part of the day and the other tribes joined in to help the Seasons to dig and sow.

The research party had arranged to stay at least over night in New Earth in order to monitor the impact of their work on the river ecosystem. They were not in a rush to finish. It was important that the plan was executed correctly and without any danger to any of the team.

Tents were established and camp fires started. The evening was spent with everyone excitedly discussing the day's events and in anticipation of the next day. Messagepads were being filled with measures and other information to be shared with the Alpha Light Matrix. Many people were watching their work from back home with high expectations. Communication was difficult with the background sandstorm picking up so people quickly retreated inside for shelter.

Kalto was occupied by picking the sand out from under his finger nails. He looked up as Inalia entered and he blushed self-consciously.

"Don't we sometimes wish we could be like the Seasons," Inalia teased as she looked at Kalto digging the sand out.

"What are they doing?" asked Bethanor curiously. He looked over from the corner of the room where he was quietly sketching ideas for his next sculpture.

"They're only sitting outside talking and playing their

instruments in the middle of the sandstorm! Given their capacity to adapt to the natural environment, it looks like their eyes are covered with a sort of transparent film barrier which doesn't let the sand through. Looks rather like egg white if you ask me. Its very strange!" added Inalia.

"It would have been so cool to have seen them in the river," said Kalto "Do you think they really develop scales? That's what I heard."

"I hear that they've come all the way from the Western plains of Reviathan to help us," said Bethanor "Although there are already quite a number of them working here in New Earth to regenerate areas of land. They're the only ones who can adapt to the harsh climate."

"Figures," said Kalto "Do you think they can teach us to do that?"

"Who knows," said Bethanor

"What a day!" sighed Inalia "I'm exhausted!"

She paused for a moment. "I'm so glad we could be here today, together," she said to her friends. "Thank you for believing in this dream, that it was possible to help, even just a little."

Both Kalto and Bethanor smiled.

"Let's see tomorrow if it worked," said Kalto "Anything might grow from that stuff overnight," he added chuckling to himself.

The three settled down to sleep with the whistling sound of the sandstorm echoing in the background.

As the sun rose over the banks of the river, they heard a call from outside the tent. People were speaking loudly, huddled over one corner of the tended land. The friends quickly threw on jackets and other protection before hurrying outside to see what the commotion was all about. There were two Season tribesmen who seemed to be crouched over investigating what looked like more footprints. It was clear that someone had been here to investigate what they were doing.

"They were definitely here last night, probably somewhere between 3 and 4 a.m.," said one of the Seasons. "It is likely there were two of them, one man, one woman. The woman seems to have crouched down to touch the land."

"Most strange," said Fenrick who had by now crouched down next to the Seasons to investigate. "I had heard that there were people here in New Earth but thought it was a myth."

Ellianon and Castedon had joined them and were looking on inquisitively.

"We've seen prints before," said Ellianon, "But I've never actually seen anyone they belonged to in all my travels. Whoever they are, they don't appear to stick around for very long."

"Well," added Fenrick "I'm not sure that it is wise for us to stick around for another night either without knowing more. Let's get going with our tests so that we can head back to Reviathan before dusk. We can monitor a number of measures from a distance over the coming days."

As the Seasons looked over the quality of the land and discussed the regenerative properties of the Halpion, the measures started to be collected. The acidity of the land had reduced dramatically. The water from the river was testing relatively clear, although the toxicity had increased by a slight amount. This meant that either it was seeping into the river from the plants themselves or from another source further upstream. The black lesions in the plant vines were starting to close over and heal. The rayadon gases that they had been emitting were no longer present in the air around the banks of the river. The encampment was rife with excitement. They had cleared the toxicity from a 3 kilometre stretch of the river so the anticipation was high to see if there was really an impact on the Aurora Belt. Was their hypothesis correct?

According to the maps that the Eastern Suburbs researchers had made, there were at least 40 kilometres worth of plants lying at different points along the river. Teams of experts would need to make several journeys over the coming days in order to execute the same clean up plan. Volunteers made themselves known and schedules were created.

"Sorry guys, you have your Rite of Passage in three days, it's not an option for you," Fenrick announced to Bethanor, Kalto and Inalia. "But we'll keep you informed the whole way through."

Back in the Western Suburbs of Reviathan, life began once again to fall into a routine but our friends were busily preparing their presentations. News came through regularly of new areas that had been cleared and they waited hopefully for news of the atmospheric impact.

The glorious day of the Rite of Passage ceremony arrived. The Sparks community filed excitedly into the main hall, wearing bright colours and wide smiles. As always they congregated in groups, talking about their latest ideas or creations until a gong rang out to invite them to sit.

The head of committee rose from her chair and smiled benevolently at all who were present. There was a moment of silence and she then proceeded to speak.

"We say that a Spark's abilities stem from our desire to understand life more deeply. We know intimately that everything has a natural place within the structure of the universe and we therefore create with this in mind. But we also create for the good of humanity, for our love of live and its continuing evolution. We alchemise that which wishes to emerge for the benefit of all. On this day of joyous celebration, may you all remember this principle as you take your place wholeheartedly within your loving community. We wish you well."

Each Spark Younger was invited to display their work and explain where their inspiration came from and the materials they had chosen to use. There were household items, tools, works of art and other fascinating innovations. As Bethanor displayed his living sculpture, the light caught the pale green hue that he had incorporated from the Chromavelia. Using only the stable part of the mineral of course. He knew better than to try to pass anything else in front of the committee, but he was satisfied. In his adventure he had found something far more important, purpose in co-creating something bigger than he possibly could have imagined alone.

As the ceremony was coming to a close, the main door opened and Fenrick appeared. The room hushed. All eyes were focused on him.

"What better time than this to share the good news with you all," he paused as he welled up with emotion. "It's working," he announced "The tear in Aurora Belt is gradually closing."

www.ingramcontent.com/pod-product-compliance
Lightning Source LLC
Chambersburg PA
CBHW061213170626
46809CB00003B/1344